THERE'S SO MUCH I NEED TO SAY TO YOU

Sutton Tell

 FriesenPress

Suite 300 - 990 Fort St
Victoria, BC, V8V 3K2
Canada

www.friesenpress.com

www.precariouspress.com

ISBN
978-1-5255-7501-3 (Hardcover)
978-1-5255-7502-0 (Paperback)
978-1-5255-7503-7 (eBook)

1. Young Adult Fiction, Coming of Age

Distributed to the trade by The Ingram Book Company

For Sonia, my rock star
And for Bash, my greatest hit

Chapter 1

Keep Smiling at Trouble

2006

If it wasn't completely tasteless, we would've named the band The Dead Parents Society, being that the tragic loss of a parent is the one thing we all have in common. But we settled on Pause For Effect, because it better suited our indie rock chops. I'm Taryn, the guitarist, and I'm dating Shay, the bassist. She's the twin sister of Nelson, our drummer. Two of us are dating and two of us are siblings, and Parker, well, you'll come to learn, Parker is an island of one.

I occasionally stick my head out of the curtains to see how the house is filling up. Our high school put on an adaptation of Sondheim's *Into the Woods* last week, and the half-struck stage is still giving off a sinister fairy-tale

1

vibe. It's the perfect ambience for a metal band's set but perhaps a little too dramatic for our indie band's sound. The Battle of the Bands will go on despite the dilapidated plastic plants lining the wings. Even though I begged my mother and sister not to come, a part of me wishes that they were here now.

Three of us drag our equipment backstage but Parker moves efficiently past us, careful not to actually unload any gear. He never does any of the heavy lifting, he's too preoccupied with keeping his over-styled spiky faux hawk intact.

His piercing green eyes are pinned on me as I mouth *"asshole"* to him. He sticks out his bottom lip. "I'm sorry I'm not carrying anything," he says in an imitation toddler voice.

I flip my hair. "Why don't you *actually* apologize to us?" I break eye contact with him and gesture at Shay and Nelson.

Parker does a double-take and then changes the subject. "That's a good color on you." He points at my shoulder-length locks. I have a habit of dying it a different color every few months. Sometimes the change is subtle, and other times it's dramatic. Sometimes there's a theme: each December, I alternate between bright blue highlights for Chanukah and screaming siren red with a lone green streak for Christmas. Today, it's lavender for no reason whatsoever.

I smirk at him while playing with a strand of my hair.

"I'm sorry!" He puts his hands together in prayer formation and bows to Shay and then to Nelson.

"You're so unnecessarily dramatic!" Shay shakes her head and moves her blunt bangs when they fall into her golden eyes.

She and Nelson exchange glances. It's uncanny, the way their facial expressions are nearly identical. They're the only pair of twins I know who not only celebrate their birthdays on different days but were also born in different boroughs. Shay was born in an ambulance on the way to Lenox Hill Hospital. Nelson was born in Lenox Hill. Shay was born in Brooklyn at 11:53 p.m. on February 14th, and Nelson at 12:08 a.m. on February 15th. They share the same brown locks, olive skin, and affinity for women. The only major difference is their height: Nelson is taller by five inches with his six-foot-two frame.

"Come off it, mate, it's cool," Nelson says, forgiving Parker.

I look around, trying to find something to distract me from the growing butterflies in my stomach. Nelson is throwing his drumsticks in the air in increasingly elaborate tricks—a sure sign of his nervousness. Shay has already halfway chewed through her nails. Across from us, Parker wrestles with the facade of pine trees and negotiates a spot, crouching behind one of them. He pulls the flask we were all sharing sips from earlier out of his back pocket and sneaks a sip.

I wave at Ryan, the Battle of the Bands show manager and lead singer of the metal band Noises in My Ear, but he's preoccupied and rushes by me. Ryan is kind of a big deal because Noises in My Ear already has a record deal, and all but one of the members are still in high school.

And how did they score their big break, you ask? You guessed it, last year's Battle of the Bands.

The notion that anyone but us gives a shit about our band is new. We are all—every band that competed for a spot on the roster—chasing the same thing: a record deal. We have to prove that Pause For Effect deserve the crown. If we win, we score a meeting with an A&R exec from Noise's record label.

"Hey." Shay smacks Nelson in the stomach to get his attention.

He slouches over. "Knock it off."

Shay takes my hand in hers. "You okay, love?" She bites her bottom lip, concealing a devilish smile.

I barely smile back. "Yeah."

"You sure?" She moves her hand up my arm.

"Just . . . slightly . . . nervous?" It comes out sounding like a question, as if I'm unsure about my own feelings.

"Hey," Nelson turns to face me, "they're a bunch of dolts. We're going to crush it."

Nelson's a consummate optimist and his casual, joking manner is often mistaken for a lack of seriousness. But I have always been able to depend on Nelson. Even though I am only dating his sister, he already feels like family to me.

I throw my backpack down in front of me to stake a claim to our spot, and my gay pride pin falls off in the process. I search the ground and salvage it, but the black rubber backing is lost somewhere inside my bag. I dig my fingers to the bottom, and they brush against my journal. It's tattered and bruised from years of carrying it around with me. The red color has started to fade away, and the leather cover is scarred with scratch marks. I have never revealed its contents to my friends and am not about to, but I stare at it. It seems to stare back at me. It's as if I can feel him wishing me luck through it. I inch it closer to my face and then shove it back into my bag almost as swiftly as I had taken it out. When I do, I feel the rubber pin back against my fingertips and affix my pin back on my bag.

Shay and Nelson huddle up with me behind a curtain, stage left, and we peer out every so often, just so we can see exactly what we are up against.

Shay pulls off her newsboy cap and throws it onto my bag. She has a style all her own. It's so unique you can't quite call it artsy or punk, but there's generally a theme. Today, she matched her cap with a T-shirt replicating a ripped newspaper. I look down at my ripped skinny jeans and gray cardigan. Nelson usually refers to my cardigans as "party cardys," or sometimes simply "partygans." My outfit doesn't grab people's attention like Shay's does. But then again, that's part of her irresistible charm: the ability to grab mine.

Ryan hustles over to us and gives each one of us stickers to wear on our shirts. "Right above your heart." He taps his chest. The stickers have a blue background with our band name in some jazzy white default font. We've been so busy practicing that we haven't had much time to come up with a proper band logo.

The noises in the crowd climb from subtle to sublime. Nelson, Parker, Shay, and I made a pact not to invite our parents so we could sneak in a little liquid courage. Well, by parents, I mean what's left of them. I lost my father when I was four. Parker lost his mother shortly after she gave birth to him, and Nelson and Shay . . . well, the loss of their mother is too hard to even think about.

From my vantage point, I can see that Parker's taken the liberty to indulge by taking swig after swig from the flask.

The auditorium fills up fast. Some members of the audience stamp and hoot, impatient for the Battle to begin. When Ryan walks out onstage, they quiet down and he leans into the microphone: "Deb and Peg are playing first." Every person in the audience goes berserk with enthusiasm. I scream loud from the side of the stage. Nelson doesn't flinch. He doesn't react. He peeps out from behind a fake pine tree and evaluates the crowd with the steadiness of a sniper.

"Their set is good, really good," Shay yells in my ear during Deb and Peg's second song. I nod in agreement.

Ryan introduces the next band: "And coming up to the stage are . . . the Problematics." The group shares a few high fives before they head out. They seem carefree and comfortable being there. I hope we project that same charisma.

Not a minute later, a feedback loop comes howling out of an amp, and the focus of the room shifts away from the band to the auditorium floor, where the audience is clapping hands over ears. The guitarist is fiercely restringing his guitar when another string pops. Some of the crowd laugh and the rest boo. The band exits the stage, looking dejected.

Backstage, they run to talk to Ryan, but he's shaking his head, yelling that once they leave the stage they've forfeited their spot.

Shay puts her bass around her and wears it low. She checks her strings.

"Let's get the Murderinos up on the stage," Ryan announces. Our classmates stomp their feet and the floor rattles; the room sways.

All of a sudden, I notice my weak knees. "Where's Parker?" Somewhere between the performances, Parker disappeared from his place behind the plants.

"He should be here somewhere." Shay places her middle finger on the E string.

"Don't be daft, he's around," Nelson says without even taking his eyes off the Murderinos' set. No one is quite certain why Nelson has an unwavering commitment to cultural appropriation of the Brits, using words like "bloody," "mate," and "daft." He's American, grew up in Manhattan, but right after their mom died, their dad whisked them away to live in London. He wanted them far away from NYC. They spent a year there and when they came back, Nelson was speaking like Ringo Starr and dressing in a wardrobe overflowing with Fred Perry.

The crowd loves the Murderinos. Not one person is seated. I can't discern whether my legs are shaking or if the room is just buzzing from the crowd's enthusiasm.

Ryan hurries over to us, runs his finger over his clipboard and yells, "Pause For Effect, you're on deck."

I call out, "Yeah, we're ready." Shay shoots me a quizzical look.

7

Ryan waits for the Murderinos to exit the stage. The crowd does not want to see them go—they're clamoring for an encore. He slowly walks up to the microphone, holds it for a beat to build anticipation, and then yells out at the crowd, "Come on up to the stage, Pause For Effect!"

The spotlight beams upon us. Hundreds of faces stare at us. Our friends all the way in the back are indiscernible; they look like cardboard cutouts from where I'm standing. Some people snicker, the Murderinos' fan club, no doubt. But most are gracious enough to give us newbies a tiny roar. I admit, it feels good to be up here and look out at the sea of faces. Wendy, one of our biggest fans, helps to get the crowd howling for us.

Nelson gets into position and starts rubbing his palms together. Shay strums her bass. I am so nervous that the tips of my fingers go numb.

I turn around. *"Where the fuck is Parker?"* I mouth to Nelson.

Then I see him. He is wandering aimlessly side stage left. I put my fingers in my mouth and whistle.

But when he turns his head to the side, I realize it isn't Parker.

Shay looks at me with a nervous half-smile and it jolts my gut. She warms up, her fingers dancing over the strings.

Parker lurches out onto the stage, holding the flask in his hand. He opens it and takes a dramatic swallow, then clumsily shoves the flask back into his pocket. He taps the microphone several times, his eyes half-lidded and drowsy with drunkenness.

Nelson straightens his posture behind the drum kit. He hits his sticks together as he calls out, "One, two, three, four!"

I pick up my guitar, my shield that floats in front of me and separates me from the world, my fingers find the strings, and I bust a riff that fills the auditorium with sound. Shay's fingers slide up and down the neck of her Fender. The way she's keeping the rhythm works its way through the room. Shay always knows the right notes to hit.

Nelson lays out a fast pattern, going in heavy and then finishing with a cymbal crash. He slams his head side to side. Sometimes, when we play together, we aren't just on the same page—we are the individual letters that collectively compose it.

Parker's vocals start and stop. He's going off-script, and we keep the music up but aren't sure where he's going. I give Parker a bewildered look.

He staggers slightly and the microphone narrowly misses his mouth. A wave of digital cameras are trained on us, taking photos that will be uploaded to Myspace by the end of the night, I'm sure. I close my eyes, not wanting to be party to this calamity any longer.

Ryan walks out to center stage and grabs the microphone from Parker. No one is amused, not even the crowd. Solemn faces stare at us, cursing us with their gazes for wasting their time. Parker should not be openly drinking.

Parker stumbles in a zigzag formation to the side of the stage with his hand on his mouth. My eyes widen.

"He's going to puke!" someone yells from the front row.

Every one of our classmates stares hard at him. It's hard to misinterpret their contempt for his sudden and abrupt arrival but Parker has always been happily impervious to other people's opinions of him. We've granted him a certain freedom in the shocking behavior department because he's the lead singer and that's what they do. But when he hunches over a ficus and nearly hurls chunks into it, no one is entertained. Parker contains his gagging motion. The moment passes and he's back on his feet.

"Ladies and gents," Ryan starts to address the crowd, clearly pissed off at us. In a momentary distraction, Parker steps forward to grab the mic from him and yells, "One! Two! Three!"

We launch into our first proper song. Parker's voice is echoing through the room as I dig in to my guitar. I look at him from the corner of my eye, watching how he keeps us going. Ryan gives us disapproving glances as he walks offstage but the crowd is going bananas, wilder than they have all night. Parker's antics had me convinced we were through, and yet everyone's jumped to their feet at the bellow of his voice.

Parker thrusts his hips, jumps in the air, headbangs with Nelson, and causes many hearts to stutter—I know because mine is one of them. Adrenaline is coursing through me. As our performance winds down, the crowd has become completely enamored with Parker.

"Thank you for being a great audience!" Parker yells. "We are . . . Pause For Effect!"

The crowd cheers as we exit. While we turn to make our way offstage, Ryan rushes by us and pulls the microphone from the stand. "I have decided to disqualify Pause For Effect."

Shay turns. "What. The. Fuck." She flips her tapered hair to the other side of her shoulders.

Nelson speaks up. "Even after that? We are clearly the best band here."

"We deserve to win!" I sigh.

"You disqualified the Problematics and now us? It's just 'cause you want the Murderinos to win." Shay wags her finger at Ryan and he winces. Her claim may hold some real truth.

I didn't think we would lose this way. Honestly, I thought we would win. But I am never surprised when it comes to Parker's disappointments. He never should've pulled out that flask onstage.

"We have won this Battle," Parker states, the usual arrogance spilling over his words.

"We need to win this. I cannot continue to live in the shadow of my famous-but-dead father." I clench my fists.

"Woah, mate. That's heavy." Nelson looks down.

Ryan stomps backstage and huddles up with the judges. The crowd's chants of "Boo!" echo off the ceiling and reverberate through the floorboards.

Ryan sulks onto the stage again and swiftly pulls the mic out of its stand, boring a hole through me with his stare.

"The judges have me outnumbered. Pause For Effect wins the Battle!"

Chapter 2
Golden Days

2009

Three years ago to the day, we graduated from high school, and on that day I was certain of three truths: first is that we would sign a record deal; second, that we would become obnoxiously famous; and third and perhaps most shocking, that the first two would ruin my life.

In January, Obama was sworn in as the forty-fourth president of the USA. In June, Michael Jackson, the King of Pop, died. And in August, Bill Sweeney, the CEO of Four Chords Music, invited us to a meeting.

I shoot the idea down in a group email between the band members. *No way, we can't do a deal with Four Chords.* But somehow, Parker convinces us to just go and *hear Bill out.* When Bill Sweeney summons you for a meeting, you go; and if you think walking into a pet shelter and leaving without something with a tail is impossible, try walking into Bill Sweeney's office without leaving on a leash of your own. At least, that's the reputation that precedes him.

The irony of how we caught Bill's attention is not lost on me. I'd assumed it was because I'm the daughter of Timothy Taylor, the famous guitarist of the band Timothy Taylor and the Standards, but it turns out it's Parker's reckless antics, which keep going viral, that caught Bill's eye. It's hard for me to understand why Parker is partying so hard lately. He conducts himself like an Amish twenty-something on *Rumspringa,* focusing on nothing other than misbehaving. But we aren't yet famous enough for him to break the rules. He needs to stay squarely in his lane before he blows it for us. Just a few weeks ago, he was nearly arrested for punching a photographer outside a nightclub. Nelson talked the photographer out of pressing charges, but you can still watch the video online. On the way over here today, Parker handed out rolled joints to a bunch of teens on skateboards as if he were a politician passing out flyers. The question is not "will he stop"—the real question is, "where are we going to draw the line?" Being that Parker's stunts are what got us official attention, today is not the day we will be drawing any lines.

We enter the offices of Four Chords Music, and one of Bill's three assistants ushers us past a wall of video screens playing a montage of the label's artists. The first office we pass houses a signed electric guitar that's mounted on the wall. The second office flaunts several hundred laminated backstage passes hanging behind the desk of a guy who looks like a suburban dad who moonlights in a wedding band on the weekends. And hanging on the wall of the third office is a framed poster of Timothy Taylor and the Standards.

My father and I have only one thing in common: a desire to play music in front of large crowds. My craving to strum and sing in unison with fans is unwavering. It's a dream I've hunted more tenaciously than my father chased his highs. He died of an accidental heroin overdose when I was four. Accidental—as opposed to purposeful. People must refer to a purposeful overdose as simply an overdose. If they're from a particularly shame-averse family, they might call it a heart attack instead. For what it's worth, in my family, we are not ashamed of my dad's struggles with addiction. But I still have trouble processing his untimely death. I wonder if the woman whose office we just walked past knows I am the daughter of the rock star adorning her wall.

We move down the hall until we reach our destination. "Corner office" would be a bit of a misnomer for Bill Sweeney's station—it takes up half the west side of the floor. A beady-eyed, middle-aged man in denim jeans and cowboy boots walks over to greet us. He sits down behind an executive desk that must have cost north of forty grand. Once he is settled in his chair, he leans back and crosses one leg over the other, resting his bronze leather square-toed cowboy boots atop his desk. His action crystallizes the fact that putting your feet up on your desk is a power move. The person across from you has to look at the remnants of dirt and debris stuck to the bottom of your shoes, which in Bill's case are one-and-a-half-inch heeled calfskins.

The desk is so wide that four chairs perfectly align themselves across its horizon. I perch myself at the far end and refuse to look directly at him or his boots. Instead, I affix my gaze on the only trimming his desk holds: a diamond-encrusted picture frame of a black and white photograph. It takes several gazes for me to realize that the photo is of him and his wife, not him and his daughter.

We are on the twenty-seventh floor of the building when Bill makes his last-ditch effort to sign our indie band with a post-punk vibe. Our power ballad is a direct nod to a certain eighties hair metal band, and our guitar solos are delivered without even a hint of hipster irony. Our music is the solution to the upper-middle-class problems our fans face, and I fear that signing with a label like Four Chords will scrub away any cred we've built faster than Bill can say in his Southern drawl, "Buick wants to license the third track on your album for a commercial."

My mind wanders as I stare out the window. Across the street, a fresh billboard poster is being pasted over an existing one. The old ad is for Nike, and the *do it* of the tagline is still present. The new ad is for a health insurance company, and all that is visible so far is its logo in the upper left-hand corner and the word *Don't*. From my vantage point, the billboard behind Bill's head is a conspiratorial wink from the universe: *Don't do it*. A burning sensation crawls up the back of my neck.

Bill looks squarely at Nelson and says, "I understand who y'all are and what y'all are trying to accomplish. Four

Chords will never alienate Pause For Effect's core audience, I promise."

Nelson's tongue curls out of the side of his mouth, and I think for sure he's going to tell Bill to shove off in his best Queen's English accent. Bill Sweeney is unapologetically Texan, completely old school, and is ruthless about making stars out of his artists.

But that last characteristic is the one that eclipses all the others. Nelson, the most pragmatic member of the band, the one I thought was so staunchly against the deal, convinces the rest of us to sign with Four Chords Music.

Chapter 3
Rhapsody in Blue

2011

It's been two grueling years of touring, and we've spent most of it away from home. Around month three on the road, the on-ramp to every city started to look the same. Tonight we are in Phoenix—no, Tucson, Arizona, and it's our final show. I am grateful for the success the tour has brought, but I'm exhausted and looking forward to going home and seeing my mom and my sister and spending time with Shay without Parker and Nelson in tow.

There are so many myths about being a touring band that people get wrong. They think it's all flashing lights, press junkets, private jets, and celebrities waiting backstage for the after-party, but it's more like early calls with tacky morning radio show hosts, truck stop bathrooms, and mediocre Thai food on the tour bus. And even you probably think that the VIP area at a concert is super sexy, just like in the movies. But I'm going to be honest with you, it is definitely not as hot as you may have fantasized. Is it nice to sit comfortably on plush sofas, sipping glasses of something delightfully bubbly, being able to hear each other speak, and not getting trampled for a good spot? Yes, that part is definitely nice. But the couches are usually scruffy and worn, the endless supply of alcohol usually results in someone being unreasonably sauced, and the dark corners inevitably lead to seeing something you wish you could unsee.

The VIP area is painted with a life-size mural of Timothy Taylor and the Standards, in what looks like a street artist's handiwork. My father's band's name emblazoned in twelve-foot graffitied letters is something like a nudge from the afterlife. One of the security guards reviewing credentials as we walked into the VIP area told me the venue, the Rebel Ballroom, had the mural painted just for me.

The lights cut out, and my eyes are trained on the Brodys as they walk onstage. They are our opening act, which means we have an hour and a half before we need to be onstage. The Brodys were so huge three years ago that we would've been opening for them instead, but their lead singer got caught doing cocaine in the bounce house at his kid's first birthday party and had to go to rehab. The band stopped playing while he was detoxing and the scandal cost them dearly. The Brodys are signed to our record company, and when Bill asked us to take them on the road with us, we couldn't say no.

Shay runs up to me, smiling and yelling, "I live for nights like these." She kisses me on the lips and offers me a soft smile. I inhale her light vanilla signature scent, feeling the bliss settle into my heart. She tucks a piece of my hair behind my ear before dragging me into the VIP crowd, her camera hanging from her shoulder. Shay lists her favorite passions in this order: 1) dating me; 2) playing in Pause For Effect; and 3) photography.

During our last year of high school, Shay took a photo for art class of an excavator being lowered onto Ground Zero in preparation for the construction of One World Trade Center. She accompanied the shot with a powerful essay. Her raw talent was immediately recognized by *National Geographic*, and she won the grand prize in one of its photography contests. Shay seldom mentions this achievement for one reason: her deceased mother. Nelson and Shay's mom, Mary, worked on the forty-sixth floor of the Twin Towers. It took Shay half a decade to return to the site, and when she did, her keen eye captured that award-winning shot. She might not mention her accolades, but she lets her affinity for photography be known to anyone who spends more than a few moments with her.

• • •

The Brodys take the stage, and the main floor is packed with stirring, shifting people in the general admission area. It looks like mountains of hot lava are rolling beneath their feet, and the only way to escape is to climb over each other. Security guards throw crowd surfers and wannabe stage divers back to the floor, and the Brodys slam their long hair back and forth in unison as they rip out the chorus. Halfway through the fourth song, when the lead singer is rolling all over the stage, Shay looks at me and smiles. "They're so fucking good!" She readies her camera in her hand and gets into position to take a shot. I nod at her. Even though they're doing the same routine they did last night in Newark and the night before that in Philadelphia, they're so tight today that it feels like we're hearing it all for the first time. Something happens during a set like this, when the energy is this frenetic and the music makes you feel higher than the clouds. I've felt this way at other shows, like I wouldn't need to take photos because I would never forget it, but tonight feels different. Tonight feels like maybe we do want pictures to prove it happened.

Shay slings her camera back on her arm and pushes her way past the hangers-on and wannabes to get a drink from the bar. She glances back at me flirtatiously and I sneak a smitten look in return. When she gets back, she hands me a Jack and Coke. She and I keep to a tight routine of making out and watching the Brodys, with her pausing every so often to capture a moment.

We've always been afraid of broadcasting our relationship to our fans because we're afraid that it will make the house-of-dating-your-bandmate cards come tumbling down. But here, in the darkness of the VIP section, I greedily steal a kiss whenever I get the chance. Shay must want more because she pulls me behind a wall into one of the many dark corners where no one can see us and lays me down atop a love seat. We make out like we did in high school, narcissistically, bordering on sloppy. Like I said, VIP sections are replete with sexy, dark corners, and you should watch where you put your drink.

We know the Brodys' set list by heart and they are nearly done. Shay pulls me closer and I suck on her bottom lip. My stomach dances with butterflies. I stare into her eyes as I take a breather before leaning back in, and as our tongues twist, our bodies follow suit.

We emerge from behind the dark corner, my Jack and Coke now watered down from the ice cubes, but I swig the last bit anyway. A tall woman is holding court for our tour manager, Logan, at the bar.

"And that's how I broke my coccyx bone, riding that horse in Mexico." He breaks out in uproarious laughter, as if the woman had just delivered the final punchline of a sold-out comedy show. My eyes dart to her tennis bracelet and then to her Rolex watch. She's definitely some exec's plus-one. How sexist of me—maybe she is the exec.

Nelson wipes sweat from his brow as he rushes over to meet me and Shay. "Aren't you the dog's dinner this evening?" His chin is covered with stubble, and his attire is purposefully disheveled. "Shall we, loves?" He motions to the corridor, which leads to the elevator that will take us to the backstage area. There is no sign of Parker yet, and I don't know how long we can keep going the way we're going. He was dividing his cocaine into neat little letters on our tour bus earlier, calling them out as he snorted them like a twisted toddler learning his ABCs. He snorted the alphabet twice. I have a feeling that if we don't do more to stop Parker soon, we might find him hanging out in the same bounce house as the Brodys' singer.

Shay grabs her camera bag and swings it over her shoulder as we walk to the elevator. She's wearing a Gucci T-shirt and Chucks—in contrast with my own outfit, which mostly consists of the perfect grandma sweater.

I catch Parker's glance as he walks into the hallway and wave him over.

"Does this suit make me look old?" he asks, approaching us. He twirls around, inspiring a whistle from Shay.

Like the best man to the groom, Nelson smooths out a cuff of Parker's blazer. "Nah, mate, these stitches are crackin.'"

Logan appears out of nowhere, swift as a ghost-like apparition. "Let's get our rock stars ready to hit the stage!" He jerkily motions his arms.

Parker notices me noticing Shay flip her hair and starts singing out loud to himself, "*You're my obsession.*" I serve him a disapproving look. Ironically, it is his own obsession with me and Shay that causes everything in our band to border on unbalanced. If not us, it'll be some other preoccupation that will cause him to come unhinged. He is constantly waging a war none of the others are fighting, and it's evident lately in his excessive indulgences and snide remarks about me and Shay. Tomorrow, it will be something new.

Logan taps his watch. "Okay, let's get moving."

"Yes, sir," Parker yells. "Just let me get a little alcohol in me."

I shoot Nelson a glance and he looks down.

Parker approaches the bar, waits impatiently for thirty-seven seconds, and then walks behind it and pours himself a Scotch, neat.

The bartender, who has no problem stealing Steve Martin's look directly from the movie *The Jerk*, asks, "Would you like to take the bottle instead?"

Logan walks over and nods to the bartender, indicating that Parker's presence behind the bar should not be tolerated.

"You know what Martha Graham thinks?" Parker raises his glass. " 'The only sin is mediocrity.'" He downs the glass in one gulp, reaches over to pick up the bottle too.

"Come on! We don't have much time!" Logan flags down one of the venue's security guys, who then escorts us down a long hallway. The floorboards have dings and missing paint from years of crews loading and unloading equipment. The walls are decorated with black-framed poster after black-framed poster of past concerts. The fluorescent lighting overhead makes the hall feel more like a school cafeteria than a music venue.

Logan crams us into the elevator. "Time is dwindling; we should have been backstage fifteen minutes ago," he shouts. He pulls the bottle from Parker's hand and runs out to put it back on the bar. Parker repeatedly presses the button to close the elevator doors—closing out Logan. The CCTV flat screen inside the elevator is on a delay, and we watch the last few moments of the Brodys performing their last song. Parker lights a cigarette, causing the elevator to come to a jarring halt between floors.

The Brodys finish their set and get the crowd rowdy with a final "Thank you, New York Fucking City!"

"I have something I need to say." Parker drops his cigarette but picks it back up and takes a drag.

"Mate, c'mon." Nelson says in an utterly charming cadence.

"No, stop!" Parker denies him in a way that a kid denies another kid a chance at his toy.

Shay and I simultaneously sigh louder than a deep exhale after good sex. "Here we go." My anxiety is palpable.

On the screen I see the roadies clearing the stage. The CCTV must be on at least a minute's delay. We really need to get backstage.

Shay unstraps her bag and pulls her camera out. She grabs a measurement of the light by facing the camera up and then down quickly. Maybe she's readying the video in case we need recorded proof of Parker's vagaries.

Nelson's smile slowly fades to a frown; he's seemingly subdued by our predicament.

"Parker, put out the cigarette." I speak as if I am negotiating a hostage situation. "We can talk after the show."

"I want to put out a solo album." Parker shimmies his hands at us. "Yeah, I said it." He giggles drunkenly. "Solo." He elongates the word: "Soooolowwwwww."

The only thing that's more uncomfortable than making awkward small talk in a cramped, immovable elevator is trying to talk about something very close to your heart with an obliterated drunk.

Nelson lifts the emergency phone off the hook. "Bullocks, totally dead."

Shay's eyes are trained on Parker.

"You know every famous singer does it." Parker stops and stares skyward.

Shay smiles widely and points at Nelson. "You want to get him in order?" She shakes her finger at her brother.

The chatter on the elevator seems to dull into a whisper as I start to fidget in the tight space. The heels of my wing-tipped Oxfords squeak on the elevator floor as I twist my feet.

Nelson scrunches his face. "That sound's bending my ear."

"This must be how Courtney Love feels when she walks into a church." I realize everyone is staring at me and willing me to cease my movements.

Shay looks down at her camera and begins to adjust the settings. She wants to take the opening shot of Parker walking out onstage tonight to memorialize our last show of the tour.

"I know you've had too much to drink," I say to Parker, "but I must admit I am growing a little tired of this script." I am calm but direct.

"Look, all's I'm just saying is, we could do better, we owe it to the fansssss to put out as much of ourselves as possible." Parker points at me, then Shay, and finally Nelson. "Don't you want our fans to be happy?" He whispers.

"Our fans are happy, mate."

"Bill Sweeney supports me." Parker drops his sentence like a grenade. He steals a look at me and the hair on my arms stands up as he narrows his eyes.

"You've spoken to Bill about it?" I ask pointedly.

Nelson interrupts, "Let's not entertain this nonsense. What song are we closing with?"

"I'm very sorry. But I want this!" Parker's losing his fine motor skills slowly and all at once.

"We are not completely prepared for this conversation right now," Shay chimes in.

"What song are we ending on?" Nelson repeats loudly, his eyes intently fixed on Parker, who doesn't answer. There is silence for a few seconds.

"Listen," Nelson brings his voice down a few notches, "let's not insult each other or the fans. Let's just go play." His words soothe me.

I turn my attention back to the screen just above Parker's head. The backdrop for our set is launched.

"Let's end tonight with the *I'm leaving the band* song," Parker says, keeping the provocation going.

"Are you fucking kidding me!" I yell in startling decibels. My words bounce off the elevator walls and stop when they hit the metallic grating on the floor.

"Oi! Everybody stop! Parker, stop it!" Nelson is becoming the personified representation of road rage. Heat is practically steaming off his head.

Parker looks up at Nelson, trying to look innocent following Nelson's sudden anger. "Okay, sorry," he whispers. "Sorry." He slides sideways.

I shake my head. Shay accidentally snaps a photograph at Nelson's utterly tangled expression, and the soft click breaks the silence.

"You are lucky this tour is over," I say tersely.

Nelson looks uneasy (camera snap), then startled (camera snap) and finally, worried (camera snap). He speaks up. "If nothing else, we know that when he sobers up, he will remember none of this."

The elevator is becoming smaller and smaller, spinning worse than the last time I did Jägermeister shots.

"It's not the point," Shay says with guttural indignation.

Nelson takes a deep breath.

"*There's just so much I want to do,*" Parker sings out.

"Well, you are doing a good job of destroying your liver, possibly our band, and definitely our friendships. Have I forgotten anything?" I look at Shay.

"He's truly one of a kind." Shay responds.

"So, we'll finish the conversation after the show?" Parker stomps out his cigarette.

"Fuck you." I turn my back to him.

The elevator shakes to life again, and we each bounce a little in place before it finally descends. Nelson drops his face into the palms of his hands, and then he runs them over the top of his head to smooth his hair over. I grab Shay's hand for a moment. When we finally hit the ground floor, four security guards and Logan are waiting to usher us to the backstage area. Shay takes a photograph of Parker as he runs onstage.

Exchanges between the band used to be musical. There was a rhythm and a melody about them. Parker's fulfilled every band singer stereotype, including being self-absorbed and flaky. Perhaps letting Parker do whatever he wanted was our first mistake. We've danced around him for years when we should have been putting our foot down.

Is Parker unbalanced? Yes. Is his execution deplorable? Absolutely. Does this feel like the approach we'd expect Parker to take—also yes. This epilogue to our tour is completely unexpected, and yet entirely unsurprising. Most people don't know when they are having their last show with their band, or a last drink with their spouse before they file for divorce, or one final cigarette break with a coworker before they drop dead. But as I look deep into Parker's eyes, I suspect this is just that. The realization of this finality sends my thoughts racing into an utter tailspin.

When everything falls apart, people like to trace it back to one specific turning point. But it's never that simple. It's a series of events, one stacked against the next like the sequential fall of dominoes—not a single piece of wood pulled out swiftly in a game of Jenga. And yet I already know I will be able to trace back my decline to this very moment.

Chapter 4

At the End of the Road

Our tour bus idles in the parking lot of the Rebel Ballroom. Logan ushers us onto it after canceling our post-concert meet and greet.

The bus is shrouded in the stench of touring, a reality of living on the road. I sit on an expensive black couch that Parker wanted even though it cramps the space. He'd insisted on ordering two hand-sewn Italian leather lounge chairs. Nelson, Shay, and I acquiesced to the purchase. We three always seem to submit to Parker's preposterous demands. I scroll my feed to see if the word is out in the Twitterverse that we canceled the meet and greet and if our fans are making noise, but nothing yet. With finally a moment to talk, none of us are speaking. We sit in a tense silence for a while, mulling over how to tackle Parker's newest stunt as he nonchalantly rummages through his suitcase. The anxiety is bubbling in my body.

Parker meets my eyes, already a weed vape in his hands, smoke billowing out from the tip. He finally says the words: "I'm leaving the band." I search his face for any hint of a joke, but his piercing green eyes reveal his sincerity.

"This is because of the solo album conversation in the elevator?" Nelson asks. He is still the band's pulse; Shay, its passion; and me, I am its beating heart. But Parker, well, Parker is the Freddie Mercury to our Queen—brilliantly talented—and without him, our band will bite the dust.

Parker slams his suitcase shut and flings a T-shirt onto his bed. Our bunks are small coffins with miniature curtains that offer very little in the way of privacy. I slide off the couch and sink to the floor. Nelson puts out his hand to help me up, but I reject it.

In the beginning, during our Battle of the Bands days, being over-the-top famous was truly my North Star. In fact, I thought it might be my only guiding principle. And I could always rely on Parker to share that with me. We sold out every venue and hundreds of fans greeted us in every city. It all started to become one big blur of success. But Parker's guiding principle slowly changed to giving in to as many desires as he had, far eclipsing my thirst for fame.

"Taryn?" Parker's shimmering eyes are pinned on me.

Parker can bring out either the lamb or the lion in a person depending on which way he switches his charm, but there will be no dignity in being a lamb right now.

"You unimaginable bastard." I squint my eyes at him, pleading with him not to do this to us. Not now, not as we're coming off this successful tour, not as our album is on the verge of going Gold.

Parker's eyes widen slightly at my comment. He opens his mouth to say something but is interrupted by the bus door opening. It's Logan. He's holding up bottles of champagne, presumably to celebrate the end of a successful tour, but it's really more of a peace offering, a diversion even. He is met with a thick silence. All of us stare at him, irritated at the sudden intrusion. He quietly sets the bottles down near the table.

As Logan stands there awkwardly, Nelson breaks the ice. "It smells like bloody death in here!" He grins as if that will make it all better.

"That's because Pause For Effect just died." I crack a bitter joke because it helps force back the tears that desperately want to escape their ducts.

Parker cocks his head back, laughing agitatedly at my comment. Shay tilts her head down and looks at me through her lashes. Only she knows how to ask if you are okay without saying a word. She turns to Logan and speaks softly. "We are kind of having an important conversation. I'm really sorry, but could you give us a moment?"

Logan takes Shay's suggestion without any hesitation and bustles toward the door. "I'll be back a little later." The tour bus door flies open and he rushes out.

"This is ominous." Nelson pulls the cork from a bottle of champagne. It hardly feels like a celebration. I fiddle with a red Solo cup and place it in front of me, not really interested in drinking but interested in the escape. Shay sits down next to Nelson, who hands his sister a cup.

Parker remains standing as the rest of us clink cups. "I'm leaving the band," he says again, an unarguable fact.

Shay keeps a decent poker face, intently focused on taking a sip.

With his trademark calm demeanor, Nelson simply says, "I think we can come to a compromise—let's talk this out." He gives a small sigh. I think even he's struggling with what it could mean for us if Parker actually leaves.

There are cords, picks, and strings littered across the black leather couches; Parker moves the gear to one side and sits down. He stretches out his legs, taking up as much space as the narrow lounge allows. I put my drink down on the floor in front of me and contemplate whether he is being serious this time. Parker is nothing if not melodramatic about even the slightest of offenses. He once had a meltdown because someone put the wrong wattage light bulb in his green room. His lack of theatrics about this bombshell has my stomach acid frothing.

"Let's knock off all the razzmatazz." Nelson pours himself more champagne.

"I can't believe we are having this conversation," Shay says in a tone that borders on a whisper. But she must believe him. "When did you decide this?"

"Bloody how? How could you do this to us?" Nelson asks.

Parker's response is as satisfying as drinking champagne from a red Solo cup. "I've been thinking about this for a while and I really want to do a solo album."

"It's a bucket list item?" I ask him, trying to discern how important this is.

"It's a dream. One I am no longer afraid to chase." He gives me a soft grin. "And I have, of course, been drinking." He winks at me as if letting me in on a little secret. "But the alcohol is not why I'm leaving, it's just what gives me the courage to finally admit it to you all."

"Well, that explains a lot," Shay says, seemingly relieved by his drunken confession.

"That explains nothing," Nelson retorts.

I sit and stare at the floor. When you witness your best friend's illicit thievery of something so close to your soul, you can't find real closure with a conversation. Maybe I'd find it by pushing him in front of a double-decker tourist bus on Broadway. Or perhaps by learning that he had a bad case of oral herpes that didn't actually cause him any pain, but flattened his self-esteem just enough to matter. Then all at once, a question drops into my mind like the Buddha's revelation, the specific and most important question to ask him, the only question that matters.

My lips quiver and my voice cracks: "Are you leaving us . . . for good?"

He opens his mouth to respond but I immediately jump back in. "Or are you *just* putting out a solo album?"

I am not sure whether his next confession makes him a courageous trailblazer or a petulant rock star.

"Both."

My face turns to stone. I have no idea what's displayed across it, but I know I'm unable to change it. The fear that we are over is infectious; it travels through me with the stinging velocity of a bullet. It begins in my skull, its kinetic energy ransacking my face. It then ricochets through my spine, penetrates my tissues, and slowly drizzles through every neuron until it pools itself in its final resting place, my heart.

Bands fall apart. Everyone knows there's always a younger, hotter version waiting to emerge from the back-streets of St. Louis or the dive bars of Detroit. But this is not that. This is one man actively working brick by brick to dismantle our band. I can't help but think of how stupid I am. How absolutely clueless I was to ever trust him.

How I wish I could go back to Bill Sweeney's office, where I sat naively with a head full of rock and roll dreams, and shout, "Don't sign the contracts! Parker's going to break our hearts!"

Pause For Effect's precipitous rise to fame shocked even us. My three best friends and I attained celebrity status just after high school. It wasn't as hard as I thought it would be—but if Parker leaves the band, holding on to fame is going to prove impossible.

Chapter 5

By the Light of
the Stars

Shay and I are headed for Montauk. The easternmost point of Long Island is best known for its beaches and its iconic lighthouse, and is accused by many of being "the end of the world" because of where it's situated. Some simply call it "the end" for short.

We've been in a heated discussion about the band for more than an hour as we drive. With Nelson's absence, we lack a band member bent on keeping things unremittingly positive. If he were here, he would insist we forge ahead without Parker. But he's not.

Shay signals an end to our continued argument: "When Taylor Swift and Kanye West kiss and make up, that's when I'll get back the enthusiasm I once held for Pause

For Effect." We marinate in silence for a minute before she changes the subject.

It's almost 9 p.m. when we reach her father's summer house. It's practically hidden amid the dense landscape of indigenous gardens and trees. We're lucky that he and his wife, Bethany, are out of the country and left the house for us to use.

Shay slowly guides the car up to the end of a long, gated driveway, the headlights revealing a modern compound of a house with windows that encompass the entire front wall. We don't waste any time; we get out of the vehicle and walk into the dark, starry night.

Once inside, a grand foyer opens up to greet us, but my gaze is immediately drawn to the country-style kitchen. I stare, mouth agape, at the rustic details and the wide wood plank flooring.

Shay stands in the doorway. She laughs at me. "It's not like you cook."

"It just looks so different from when we were last here," I exclaim.

"Yeah, they gut renovated it. Added that wall of windows over there," she says, pointing, "new kitchen, new bathrooms, wraparound deck downstairs, oh, and a new balcony upstairs."

She pulls me across the expansive open floor plan and walks me directly to the back deck. I am nearly delirious with happiness as she opens the doors. I audibly gasp at the sight of it. She squeezes my hand as if to ask, *can you believe this view?* From my vantage point, all I see is a private footpath leading to the beach, with waves set against a pitch-black night.

"You can go see the upstairs if you'd like," she smiles, and I follow her instructions.

The second landing is hot and muggy. On the far back wall, a five-foot framed still of the Twin Towers catches the corner of my eye, and I must surrender to its gravitational pull. Shay says that she will be right up, she is just going to turn on the central air. I dip my head into what looks like the guest suite, place my bag just inside the doorway, and hurry back to the landing to view the larger-than-life image.

I inch closer to it with the precision of a patron on an art crawl, hands behind my back. Its presence hits me like a smack to the gut. I stand several feet from it, which is the proper distance one needs to truly take it in. Its enormity is not only tasteful, which is near impossible to pull off, but loaded with indescribable emotion.

Shay sneaks up behind me and it's not her presence that startles me but her words: "From the moment the planes went barreling into the Twin Towers, Nelson and I have been emotionally on our own." She motions with her chin to her father and stepmother's bedroom. "It's not that I don't like her—Bethany—she's great as far as stepmothers go. She's actually very sweet." I watch her eyes linger over the photograph of the building that represents the passing of her mother, a sad smile on her face. Then I follow her into the master bedroom. She heads purposefully over to a framed picture on the dresser of her, Nelson, their father, and Bethany, standing in front of his private equity firm, Fitzgerald, Hughes, & Langworthy. The letters *FHL* are prominent behind them.

Shay flips the frame over and places it back on the dresser, right-side down.

"She's . . . just not my mom . . ." Shay is intense and passionate, yet measured with her words.

I grab Shay's hand to comfort her. "I know the agony of a missing parent."

There are two universal truths about life, which I've accepted under protest. The first is that time passes, and the second is that everybody dies. The latter produces heaviness within me that I have skillfully learned the art of shaking off. As time passes, the people you love die again and again: when you think of them, when you see their photograph, when you hear their laugh in a crowd. Grief and love are intermixed. The pure light of love doesn't come without the darkness of grief. And among other things I've learned, it's that life is sometimes not fair.

I pull Shay's arm and we head back downstairs. In the kitchen, she takes a bottle of wine from the wine fridge and directs me to grab two glasses. We reconvene on the back deck to enjoy the staggering views of the sea and sky. The night air is crisp. She pours us each some wine and we clink our glasses together.

Each tree yields a unique symphony—a swish of the wind here, a chirping of a cricket there—and the enchanted sounds of the dark practically lull me to sleep. My head bobs to the side and up again from over-tiredness, and the wine glass nearly slips from my fingers. When Shay notices, she leads me up to our bedroom, tucks me into our bed, and kisses me on the forehead like a parent does to her sleepy child.

• • •

When morning breaks, the sun drenches me. Yawning, I reach for one of the pillows and reposition it. I hear the ocean's noises and lift my head toward the window to wrap my ears around the sounds. Shay is standing by it, staring out, her back to me.

She turns around to face me and gives me a wry little smile, her olive skin sun-kissed from the rays. She quickly turns back again to look out at the beach.

It seems like a long time before one of us says anything or changes position. She breaks our silence—"Stay there, don't move"—she grabs her camera.

She takes what feels like hundreds of pictures of me—pausing every sixty seconds to glance down and review the photos before starting again. When she stops to change the lens, I collapse into the pillow, my arm on my forehead.

"Hold it—do not move," she demands as she stands at the end of the mattress, straddling my feet, taking the shot from above. "You look patently gorgeous." She puts the camera down after examining the photos.

"Did you get the shot?" I laugh.

"Oh, I got it all right." She cups my face in her hand. "Let's head down to the beach. We shouldn't waste another moment inside." She rushes down to the bottom of the stairs with a beach bag slung over her shoulder and waits for me.

Once we find the perfect spot, Shay unrolls her beach towel. I still have mine draped around my neck like one wears a wool scarf in winter. I battle with the wind to lay my towel down in a straight line, and eventually, I win. I settle my head back and let the sun shine on my face.

• • •

"I think I am keeping myself purposely detached from finding another singer." I'm bringing the subject back to the band. "I am afraid that any band we start without Parker will ultimately end up as someone else's good fortune again."

"I think it's time we all start living for ourselves and stop worrying about Parker." Shay reaches her arm out for my hand. "Let's go in the water."

The temperature is shockingly cold at first, but I plunge underneath to even it out. Shay dips underwater and emerges a moment later, her hair slicked back, her golden eyes, gorgeous.

No sooner then we get back to our spot to dry off does a woman from a neighboring house stroll along the beach. I secretly wish for her to keep going, but she walks up to us, waving.

"Shay!" You look exactly like when you were younger," she laughs. "I would recognize you anywhere." She says to me, "I'm Catherine," as I wring my hair out. I wave at her.

Catherine has a real hippie feel to her. She wears a red bandana that barely tames her wild hair. Her weathered face is a representation of the many lives she's undoubtedly lived, and lived well. I learn that she lives two houses down. She's known Nelson and Shay since they were children, apparently, so obviously, she knew their mom. And she gets along with Mr. Hughes and Bethany very well. So well, in fact, that "when Bethany mentioned Shay was coming, I was hoping I would bump into you. I haven't seen you or your brother since you were this big." She puts her hand up against her left hip to demonstrate.

I can sense Catherine's a real spitfire. She insists we make small talk with her, rattling off quick questions. She talks fast and has a lot to say, but barely allows us to respond. Eventually, I join Shay on our beach towels, curling my knees up to my stomach and then releasing them. Catherine sits down next to us, either ignoring or not caring about our blunt move away from the small talk. My foot starts shaking uncontrollably. Shay looks down at my knee and places her hand on it. One of my fantasies with Shay begins exactly in that position. My foot stops.

Catherine goes right for the jugular. "Let's get the Pause For Effect elephant out of the room." She waves her hands in the air. "So, what happened?"

My shoulders collapse.

Shay shakes her head side to side. Then she stands straight up, walks over to her bag, and takes out her camera.

"The light is perfect." She holds her camera in her right hand. "I have to take a few shots before a cloud moves in." And she leaves me, just like that, alone with this rich hippie neighbor person who has absolutely zero appreciation for social cues. I throw Shay a menacing look.

If you've ever suffered a broken heart, then you know that memories work strangely, particularly when you process pain. Memories do not work in a linear, filing cabinet fashion as we all think they do. Insidious flickers of recollections blindside you and bring to the forefront moments you didn't even realize you'd filed away in the first place.

Catherine drones on and on about Pause For Effect. There's something about the way she pronounces it—she doesn't say it in four syllables, but in a swift, monosyllabic way, "pauseforeffect," like she's learning a new language and is embarrassed to pronounce it appropriately because she feels like an impostor. It makes my eyes start to water a little, suddenly, just thinking about the name.

I tune out, preoccupying myself with clearing excess sand off my towel. Catherine slams the palm of her right thigh and a loud clap rings out, bringing me out of my daze, and she laughs at something she said. I finally grow impatient and tell her that we have committed our time and are running afoul of our predetermined schedule. Whatever that lie means.

Almost as oddly as it started, our small talk assault ends and Catherine continues walking down the beach. She waves goodbye to Shay, but Shay is more concerned with chronicling the entire day behind her camera than experiencing it. Her musical prowess is effortless, intuitive almost, but she wears her camera more than she wears her bass lately. She crawls on the sand to get her shots. You can tell when she gets a good one—her face illuminates like a young child who's walked into a toy store for the first time.

Shay joins me back on the towel and puts her camera back into its bag. The yellow sun sinks behind the horizon, and we agree it's time to head back to the house.

My small footsteps are inaudible on the expanse of the second floor. I hurriedly take off my clothes, anxious to see if Shay will follow me into the shower.

When she and I leave the shower, I dip into the master suite and flip the family photograph back over on the dresser. The foursome of Nelson, Shay, their father and step-mother is straight out of central casting; they come through as American as apple pie. I hesitate for a brief moment, wondering if Shay will want me to keep it as she left it.

She doesn't seem to care either way. Shay peels off her wet towel before joining me in bed, her eyes on mine. Teasingly, she stays a good distance away, gently drying her hair with a towel.

"Shay," I whisper softly, reaching my hand out to her. I don't mind showing how desperate I am for her touch.

She straddles me, looking like an absolute vision above me. She slowly pulls off my towel, the smile never leaving her lips. I raise my hips to her. I trace the nape of her neck with the fingers of my left hand. Her velvet tongue gently caresses every part of my body. We are completely in sync, melting into each other like clocks in a Dali painting.

We lay together, cuddling. Shay's chest rises and falls gently with each breath she takes, and I lie still on her heart center, falling deeper and deeper into the rhythmic beat, as if hearing it from the inside of her chest. She is softly drawing circles on my shoulder with her finger.

"I have something I need to ask you." She removes her hand from my shoulder to play with her ring. She tends to pull it on and off her finger whenever she is curious about something.

"Words every woman wants to hear after sex." I smile, but she has a hard time keeping her eyes on me, and my smile quickly fades.

"What's our future hold?" She cocks her head curiously at me.

I instinctively sit up and pull the blanket up to my chest.

I marvel at the greediness of her timing.

"Us as in us, or us as in the band?"

"Taryn, honey, I hardly care about the band at this point."

"Well, for us, I mean, you are my future." I grab her hand and clasp it in mine.

"Do you see marriage in our future?"

"Of course I do." I kiss her hand.

"And children?"

I drop it back down. We've loosely had this conversation before.

"Are they in our future, yes. Is that future imminent, no."

"I feel about children the way you do about the band."

"That you want to get them . . . back together?" I laugh.

"That my future is nothing without them."

I shift. My stomach churns. I draw in a deep breath. "My priority is music right now. Can we commit to that together?" I pick up her hand again and hold it inside both of mine.

"I have a plan—things I want to get done before I have children—and I feel very passionately that I want to experience these desires before times move too fast and passes me by." She holds my hand lightly, knowing I could pull it back at any time, but I do not.

"Well, like what?"

"I want to travel."

"We've seen the whole country, and Europe, and when the band gets back together we'll see the whole world."

"After a while, on tour, every skyline starts to look the same. I want to see villages and beaches, children, and churches. I want to photograph more than just Parker jumping out onstage."

"What are you saying, Shay?"

"I know what I want my future to hold." She squeezes my hand. "It's you, it's marriage, it's children with you."

I slowly exhale. "And on that, we are absolutely connected, honey."

"It's just what I want to do before we get there." Her eyes transfixed on me.

"Okay, so we get the band back together, and we work in more time for travel, and for us."

"I think I want to leave the band and build up my photography portfolio."

"But why do you need to leave the band? It's the exact opposite of what I'm trying to achieve. I'm trying to get Parker back. I can't play whack-a-mole with my band members."

She exhales loudly. "I want to take a break, build my portfolio, and travel, full stop."

I have never seen her come so undone.

"Will you"—the tears come pouring down her face—"will you come with me or not?"

I pause but words don't come out.

"Come with me," she begs. She doesn't look me in the eyes as she starts to busy herself with getting dressed.

"But you don't even like professional photography. You think gallery owners are pretentious and coffee table books are too posh."

"That's not the point."

Though the room is impeccable save for my wet towel on the floor, the immaculate space suddenly has a forsaken feel to it.

My thoughts are scattered—I can't look at her—I move my gaze to the vivid beach. The fuzziness of my mind impairs my vision. I can no longer tell where the sky begins and the ocean ends.

"Shay, I can't just pick up and travel around the world for a year watching you take pictures."

"Why can't you? It's the perfect time for it."

"Well, first of all, I don't have your trust fund."

That was low, and I know it immediately. I regret the words before the sentence is halfway out of my mouth. I have never once brought up the fortune Nelson and Shay have acquired as a result of their mother's death. And in fairness, my own more modest dead-parent stash could probably afford me the chance to gallop around the globe with her. But—but that's not the point. The point is, I shouldn't have said it.

We are both silent. I don't know what to do or say.

"I just want to travel for a year. And the fact that you will not come with me is—"

"Don't call me selfish. Don't you dare call *me* selfish."

"I thought you wanted to be with me?" She grabs hold of my face with both hands and leans in to kiss me. She's mad, but she's magic. There's no mistaking her passion. Our mouths align, as does every curve of our bodies. *But kissing her now is crazy!* I plead with myself. At the very least, it's close to the border, inching toward where sane and insane intersect.

"Taryn, live in the moment. Everyone else is. Parker is. Nelson is. We should too."

"We have the band."

"Had."

"I'm going to get Parker to come back." I tilt my head at her.

"Good luck getting him back. If you do, it'll have more strings attached than a Beethoven symphony."

My head spins as I stand up. I feel myself sway slightly, more from emotion than anything else. I open my weekender and pull out a T-shirt and a pair of shorts.

"I am asking you—please—join me on a once-of-a-lifetime journey." Shay stands up and inches toward me, grabbing for my waist.

"I am asking you—please—do not be the nail in Pause For Effect's coffin." I move back a few steps.

"Do you care more about me or the band?"

Her words ring in my head.

"I care more about . . ." I pause.

She shakes her head and slowly heads toward the door.

"That's not why I'm pausing! I'm pausing on how to refer to you: my lover, my girlfriend, my best friend? Dare I go so far as to say ex-girlfriend?"

The tastemakers who decide on witty, catchy ways to describe romantic situations like ours haven't yet coined a proper term for bandmates who fall deeply in love with each other, love them so much that they selflessly let each other go. Do the bloggers have a name for that yet?

Shay stops at my words and looks back at me. "Oh, stop it. I'm your girlfriend. But please, you need to support me now. It can't all be about you, or Parker, or this fucking band!"

"Even though you are definitely *the* best thing about my life, I don't think I have the luxury to take this step with you." I speak softly. "Traveling around for a year means that we'll have to uproot whatever remains of the life we have here."

"But Taryn, this *is* our lives, our future, and I need you to be a part of it."

"And what if I don't go"—I stumble on my words—"are we broken up, are we sleeping with other people, what does that even look like?"

"Sleeping with other people?" She abruptly stands up. "Wow, you went there fast."

"No—" I stop. "I mean," I try to stop her from walking out, "I just meant—"

"Something about me you've never appreciated is how I read the room. It's why I'm made for being a photographer." She raises her hand and touches my chin gently to turn my face toward her.

With guttural indignation, I push her hand away. "I can't figure out if I wish I had never met you or if I praise the day I set eyes on you."

"See, it's all black and white, good and evil, bad and worse with you. It's not a journey, it's not living in the moment, and it's not the experience. It's the possession. You do it with our band too. You just want everything to belong to you. Me, I enjoy the opportunities, each one. No moment is fixed in the stars, so I enjoy it for what it is. And sometimes, I am so bold as to capture it."

The tears bleed from my eyes in the form of what I feel for her, feelings I thought were more than just a symphony of heavy breathing that escaped our lips at 3 a.m.

She gives a final nod, keeping her eyes on mine as if sealing a deal, before turning around to walk away.

I don't remember how we managed to get through the remainder of the night. I remember clutching each other through our tears several times after our conversation about her leaving to travel to nowhere in particular and everywhere at once. I remember killing several bottles of Sancerre. I remember my smile leaving me as I realized another band member was going to disappear on me—and this time it was my love, my family. And I remember waking up the next morning crying, thinking that I could do whatever I wanted and nothing at the same time. Thinking that my stupid inaction might lead me to lose Shay forever.

Chapter 6
Show Me the Way to Go Home

The sign that heads off my mom's street reads, *Dead End*. It's eerily appropriate for how I'm feeling. The drive from Montauk to Forest Hills, Queens, is exactly two hours, twenty-two minutes, and thirty-nine seconds. I know because my older sister, Gwen, reminded me several times how long the drive was before agreeing to pick me up.

"I owe you, I know, I know," I repeated to Gwen when she showed up at Shay's dad's house to taxi me to our mom's place. Shay was taking a walk on the beach when Gwen arrived, and honestly, it was better that way.

Our childhood home is a terra-cotta-shingled Tudor-esque home that Mom's realtor friend once described as a "European fairy-tale castle." When Gwen pulls up into the driveway, we wave at Mom's neighbor Mr. Kelsey. He's standing in front of his house, smoking a cigarette. He's lived next door as long as I can remember, and he's sort of a grump. He's a handy type, always busy with some sort of manual labor. His Saturday routine usually includes cleaning out the gutters, watering the lawn, and sweeping the sidewalk directly in front of his house. When Gwen and I were younger and left our belongings strewn about our yard, our stuff would sometimes cross over the invisible line of where our property ended and the Kelseys' began. Once an item crossed over, no matter how small the infringement, he would return it to us. The collection of things he left on our front steps included notebooks, magazines, jump ropes, and as we got older, lip gloss, iPods, earbuds, and packs of cigarettes we experimented with but never committed to.

Mom opens the front door and smiles at me as I head up her walkway. Boy, did I miss her smile. Immediately she fusses over my hair, which is apparently too short now. The ambience of her "castle" is different now than when I lived here nearly half a decade ago, but it's hard to say why exactly. Mom left our old bedroom completely untouched, so it has become something of a nostalgic storage unit, with our father's old steamer trunk still in the closet. Every so often when I come home to visit, I unload a spectrum of items, from the sentimental to the insignificant.

Gwen throws her stuff onto the bench near the front door. When she and I were kids, we used to sit one behind the other on that bench and pretend we were on a school bus. We'd take turns being the bus driver. Gwen makes a beeline for the den and Mom heads into the kitchen. Mom's had more than a few patients cry on her couch about a breakup—I'm sure she and Gwen have already had a conversation about how to handle mine. Yeah, Mom's a shrink. Actually, "shrink" is misleading—she's a bit of an enigma. On the one hand, she's a clinical psychologist who specializes in cognitive behavioral therapy. On the other, she studies astrological charts and will advise her clients based on when Mercury will be in retrograde. And she's obsessed with Princess Diana. It's a trifecta I like to call "science meets the stars meets the royals." Knowing her, she probably attributes my breakup to a Saturn return or the phase of the moon. Or something equally absurd.

I slink upstairs to my old room and throw my weekend bag onto one of the twin beds. I open the curtains to let the sun drape the room in a shaft of light. Stiff from the sheer exhaustion of the long drive, I fall into the other bed and lie there for a few moments. I can't help but think that I have somehow managed to survive till now. *I survived.* Which is a feat, considering that at several points on that drive over, I was convinced I would die of heartbreak.

Everything looks exactly the same in my childhood bedroom, yet feels completely different. The rug under my feet has the same familiar pattern, but it's not as soft as it used to be; the walls are a faded version of the emerald green that I was once in love with as a teenager. It's difficult to feel at home in a space that you last resided in when your life was completely different. The walls, the floor, even the air betray you. The same fixtures exist here, but my whole life feels transformed.

"*Mommm*," Gwen wails, the word ripping out of her mouth at the pitch of a newborn first entering the world. "The Wi-Fi isn't working again." She's yelling from the den downstairs, but her voice carries through the vents so it sounds like she's right beside me.

"There's something about your sister's shriek that suggests a bit of regression," says Mom, startling me as she mysteriously appears in the doorway.

"I'm too tired to handle her bullshit theatrics." I dramatically pull a pillow on top of my face and hold it tight by my ears.

Mom pulls the pillow off my face and takes a seat on the twin bed across from me.

"Do you want to talk about it?"

"My big sister and her big mouth." I shake my head.

"It's because she loves you." She takes off one black heel and straightens her nude stocking.

Instead of overreacting, which is what every cell in my body wants to do, I calmly say, "Yes, Shay and I broke up."

"*Mommm*," Gwen calls again.

Mom stands up quickly, and I motion for her to go on without me.

Nestled in the corner of the room is my desk. I collapse onto its accompanying chair and stare at a blue sticker on the wall, faded from time and wear much like myself, with the words *Pause For Effect* across the top and *Battle of the Bands* across the bottom. I rip the sticker off the wall and hurl it into the garbage.

"*Taryn*," Gwen yells impatiently.

I stand up and stomp across the room, because that's what you do when your sister is shouting and everything in your childhood home feels like a regression. I shove my iPhone into my pocket and head downstairs.

The stairway wall is decorated with visibly askew pictures of our family. These are neither random nor candid—not "moment stealers," as Mom calls Instagram. These are "Taryn, go back upstairs and change; you *will* wear what I laid out for you!" family photographs. Gwen is standing at the bottom of the stairs, waiting for me, when she sees me stop to take in the pictures. She walks up the steps to look at them with me. Only half her face seems to be done in makeup, and I restrain myself from commenting on it, though I'm curious.

When my sister and I were younger, the argument about my attire rekindled once a year when the photographer Mom hired came to capture us doing *everyday* things, like jumping in tandem in the front yard or throwing leaves at each other. We did this every year until I was a freshman in high school. Mom eventually gave up and let me style myself for the photo shoots. My looks ranged from young tomboy with slicked-back hair to sporting drainpipe jeans and bright neon wigs. Gwen has worn variations of the same thing each year since she was seven years old: a dress and makeup.

"God, that dress was so awful. What was Mom thinking?" Gwen comments, laughing a little at the absurdity of the purple dress with ruffles she's wearing in one of the pictures. I laugh with her before walking down a few more steps. Taking my time to study the shots, even though I've walked by them hundreds, if not thousands of times in my life. The oldest one is a picture of my grandfather when he returned from World War II. There's my favorite photo of Gwen and me, the one where we're sitting on a branch of the oak tree in our yard.

And to the left, framed in red, is one of me playing a fire-engine red guitar for my fifth-grade talent show. I won first place. Despite the passage of time, I still live in a world in which my most treasured currency is made up of melody and hooks, raps, and riffs.

"Come on!" Gwen tells me.

On the first floor in the kitchen, Mom is cleaning Neo's cage. The floor around her African gray parrot's cage is carpeted with piles of newspapers. When she removes the blanket from overtop Neo's cage, he starts to hop with delight. *"Rauuuurrr!* Olá!" A strong gust of wind rips through the kitchen and Neo goes wild with glee, bopping his head up and down.

Mom acquired Neo by way of Fátima, a Portuguese woman who was both eccentric and beautiful—but I think that's the only way Portuguese women are built. Fátima insisted on giving Mom her bird as a gift. There were two problems with Neo: one, Mom couldn't accept gifts from patients, and two, the fucking bird only spurted Portuguese phrases. But Fátima wouldn't take the bird back because this would tap into her "fears of rejection." Then she moved back to Nazaré, Portugal, and Neo really became ours.

I walk into the perfectly disheveled den that sits just off the living room on the first floor. Gwen follows me and goes straight to her laptop screen. She pulls her hair back into a bun so tight it could give her a facelift.

"I was in the middle of recording a cat-eye tutorial and the Wi-Fi crapped out again," Gwen explains. I can see her makeup attempts more clearly in the light of the room. Her face is split down the middle by an invisible line—on one side, she's wearing a full face of makeup with some stray splotches of eyeliner, and the other reveals her naturally blemished skin.

"Cat-eye tutorial." I laugh. Gwen's gained a cult-like following for her beauty vlog, *Glamour by Gwen*. I once witnessed her weave "proper lip liner application" into a conversation at the pharmacy about a sinus infection. She graduated from Queens College, Magna Cum Concealer.

She's sitting at Mom's desk, which is buried under mountains of papers that create an abstract outline of the Swiss Alps. The shelf just above the desk is decorated with enough Princess Diana tchotchkes that something about it feels dirty. The House of Windsor cigar box is overshadowed by the creepiest collectible of them all: a Franklin Mint porcelain Diana doll.

Gwen frantically hits the space bar. "Taryn, please help me fix the internet!" Her plea is dripping with desperation.

"I love the way you refer to the internet like it's something tangible you own." I pick up the wireless router. It hangs precariously from a ball of wires like a child's loose tooth from the end of its root. "Like you could misplace the internet the way you so often do your car keys."

I motion for Gwen to get up from the desk, power off the computer, and begin to untangle blue and black wires.

I reach far behind the twenty-seven-inch computer screen. Hidden behind it is a framed photo of me, Mom, Gwen, and our father—his slicked back hair, the arrogant lift of his eyebrows, his piercing blue eyes, and signature smirk. I wipe a thick layer of dust from the glass and show it to Mom. "What did you have us dressed in?"

Mom moves her glasses down to the tip of her nose. "You were wearing thrift store clothes."

"Thrift store clothes were trendy then?" Gwen asks.

"Your father." Mom shakes her head.

Implicit in her terse reply is her disappointment with who our father really was. Gwen and I have learned over the years that he was terrible with money. So much so, Mom had to insist that when Timothy Taylor and the Standards signed their record deal, he'd get life insurance as a part of his advance. She's reminded us dozens of times that if she hadn't done this, we would've never been able to move from our two-bedroom rent-controlled apartment in Manhattan's Lower East Side to a Tudor home on a tree-lined street in Forest Hills.

The heaviness of their marriage lingers in the air even as I fiddle around with the Wi-Fi router. My head now lodged behind the screen, I snake the black Ethernet cable down the back of the desk, drop to my knees, and pull the cable down toward me.

"Gwen, hand me the router."

She hands me the external hard drive.

"No, that thing right there." I point.

"Okay, now hand me the blue cable that's right there."
Beads of sweat are appearing on my forehead.

"Honey, be careful." Mom hovers over us like an
onlooker to a car crash.

I stand up and reach behind the computer to turn it
back on. "I have, like, one memory of Dad, that's it. The
rest is just the greatest hits, stories people have told me
over the years."

"I'm sure half of them are made up at this point,"
Mom says.

"You just called him Dad. You never call him that,"
Gwen says. "*I* always call him Dad."

"It just comes out when I'm around Mom sometimes,"
I huff, and then click a few buttons. "Okay, the Wi-Fi is up
and running again."

"Okay, you guys have to get out," Gwen tells us. "I don't
want any background noise while I record."

I pick up the framed photo of the four of us from
Mom's desk, a proverbial waltz frozen in time. The truth
is, I wish that I had a living, breathing father instead of
a stand-in made of negatives and piles of photographs. I
vaguely remember this man. My recollection of the last
time I saw him is spotty, if not formed wholly out of stories
told to me by other people. Despite the loss of memories
never created and opportunities never seized, the love of
an ephemeral father is one that smacks you across the face
like a woman who's just caught you cheating. It burns no
matter what age you were when you lost him.

I often struggle with how to talk about my father. I
should not refer to him in the present tense—that much

I know. I was so young when he died that I never got the opportunity to know him, not the way Gwen did. To her, he's Dad, and it's that simple. I remember that during the wake, I tried to draw with crayons on his casket, and during the burial, while the priest was giving a sermon I had a loud and violent tantrum. One of Mom's colleagues had to calm me down because I wouldn't speak to anyone in my family. I know it's rude for me to refer to him as my father instead of my dad, but to me, a dad is someone who lives long enough to drop his kid off to her first day at kindergarten. In moments like these, when I am forced to face what I don't have any more, I am at least grateful that I have his music.

Mom leans in over my shoulder and says to me proudly, "I did a damn good job of raising you two without a man. You've got a band, and Gwen's a YouTube star."

I shoot Mom a sideways glance and put the frame back on the desk. "Star? She literally records herself as she puts on makeup."

"Hey," Gwen retorts, "your band is basically broken up, and I'm represented by Lewk Artistry."

The sound of a trap remix of the original iPhone ringtone plays from my pocket, immediately silencing the den. No one calls you anymore. In fact, according to my mother, it's rude to call someone without first texting and asking, "Is now a good time to call?" And if I'm being honest, I agree with her. So when my phone rings, it conjures an immediate swirl of panic in my gut.

I raise the phone to my ear.

"'Ello, love."

"It's Nelson," I tell Mom and Gwen. This news assuages their fretful stares.

"What's he saying?" Gwen talks over Nelson, and he hears her in the background.

"Is that Gwen?"

"Yeah, she brought me to Mom's."

"Tell her I said hi."

I put the phone away from my face and whisper to Gwen, "Nelson says hi." She waves back to me.

"I heard the news," Nelson goes on.

"You spoke to her?" I ask.

"I didn't speak to her, no."

"What are you talking about, Nelson?"

"Are we talking about the same thing?"

"What's he talking about?" Gwen says over me.

I shoo her away from me.

"The article by Sofia Alexa," Nelson says.

"Oh." I pause. "I refuse to read an article by that woman."

"She's not that bad."

"Nelson, she named her company Sleaze Media. Who does that?"

"You know that's not what SLZ stands for."

Sofia, Lynda, Zoey—the co-founders of SLZ. Against all conventions, they boast an all-female executive team for their budding entertainment content platform. "Look, I appreciate their empowering agenda and I fully support women owned companies, I do." I sigh. "I just find Sofia's approach to 'entertainment news' a bit unapologetic at times."

"I thought you liked unapologetic women?" Nelson laughs.

He doesn't know how his silly comment punctures me like an arrow to my carotid artery.

"Anyway, what happened with her, Sofia Alexi?" I stand up a little bit straighter, bracing myself so the signal he's about to send doesn't knock me to my knees.

"The headline is, well . . . He says . . ." Nelson stalls.

"Nelson?"

"Well." He pauses.

I grow agitated. "Get on with it."

"Her source says Parker's dropping his first song today."

It's been nine months since Parker left the band, the span of a pregnancy, and if the rumors are true, he will birth his new solo album any day now.

"Her *source*." I laugh. "See why I don't like these content producers—this isn't journalism."

"You know Parker is a bit of an asshole, Taryn. I wouldn't put it past him to dump the rest of us like a hunter disposes of a turkey carcass."

"He already has!"

"So what news were you talking about?"

As the seconds lapse, so does the pulsation of the thick knot behind my left eye.

"Have you spoken to your sister?"

"No."

I'm silent, but confident he can hear the sound of my bottom lip quivering.

"Darling, this can't be. Not my best friend and my sister. You two are solid."

"Were," I correct his tense.

"I am so sorry, sweetie. If you need anything . . ."

"Yeah, so. I'm at my mom's while I look for a place."

"Aye. This is serious."

"Yup."

"So she's keeping the apartment?"

"Nope."

"Then why are you moving out?"

"Too many memories."

"Taryn, I don't even know what to say."

"You should probably call her. She's got loads of news to share with you."

He goes on asking question after question, his voice suddenly sharp and loud, the sound of it ricocheting like a gunshot. I'm not sure why, but I find his innocent queries insufferable. Embodying a true rock star, I throw my phone across the room. It narrowly misses Gwen's head.

Gwen and my mother stare at me in silence.

I rub my forehead and take five deep breaths.

There was once an impenetrable love between the members of Pause For Effect. There was me, and I was in love with Shay. Nelson and Parker were our best friends, and it was all innocent and grand until Parker got greedy. And like a Diabolus ex Machina, Shay just stole the show. First, Pause For Effect broke up, and then me and Shay. The heartbreak hits me like a roundhouse punch.

Gwen has this problem where she laughs when she's uncomfortable, like when there's silence in a yoga class or when she's attending a wake. "What?" Her lips curl up at the ends. Through a half-suppressed laugh, she asks, "What happened?" She giggles.

"I have to stay here." I turn to my mom and give her an apologetic sigh.

"Yes, of course, sweetie, whatever you need," she responds—and she seems to catch herself before saying more.

"No, like, I have to move in." I turn to Gwen. "I want to get this over with before Shay comes back from Montauk. Round up some men and help me move out of my apartment."

"Some men? What do you think, I have them on deck?"

Gwen treats her visits to Queens like freshmen in college treat their first Thanksgiving weekend at home. She calls everyone she knows, she parties too much, she sleeps with someone she shouldn't, and then she leaves town in a hurry. Trust me, there's more than a few men she can call.

I cock my head sideways at her.

"Ugh." She starts looking through her bag for her keys. "I'll make some calls in the car!"

• • •

We mostly stay silent during the drive back to my place. Gwen has kept her word and called in favors. I keep my mouth shut and scroll through my phone. A few miles into the drive, Parker's first single, "The Sounds of Chaos," plays on the radio, right as we're crossing over into Brooklyn. When Gwen agitatedly tries to turn the radio off, she accidentally turns the heat on full blast; she and I argue for several minutes as we both try unsuccessfully to turn it off. Even though it's a ninety-degree day in August, I would rather argue over Gwen's faulty coolant system than talk about how I am slowly coming undone.

Chapter 7
Save Your Sorrow
for Tomorrow

I've spent one hundred and twenty-seven days without Shay, and for some reason, today is the toughest. The first few weeks of being back at Mom's were weird, but then I settled into it. The milestones hit (spending my birthday without Shay followed by Thanksgiving without Shay) and time passed both slowly and quickly—some days seemed to sprint by, but sometimes, they crawled. There were days when I screamed into my pillow, and others where I cried in the shower. Most days I wouldn't leave the house, but some nights, I partied my ass off and paid for it dearly in the form of a hangover. Regardless, the minutes eventually turned into hours and the hours into days, until today,

Gwen called and I greeted her with: "I need you to come to Mom's."

She and I have this sick way of knowing the exact moment the other is crossing the tipping point. I called her exactly forty-seven seconds after she and her ex-boyfriend broke up. She called me before I even left the Four Chords building, knowing I had just signed my first record contract.

I'm lying on the couch in the den when she arrives. She hasn't even put her keys down when she starts complaining that she had to cancel her Sunday brunch plans to come and put me back together.

"I'm sorry I interfered with your eggs Benedict and mimosas." But we both know I'm not sorry—she's my sister, this is a part of what she's responsible for, it's in our sibling contract.

"Where's Mom?" Gwen looks around.

"I don't know, I'm not her keeper. Probably at, like, Costco or something."

I stand up and look out the window. It's gray and gloomy and looks like burial weather. "C'mon, let's go upstairs."

Gwen follows me up to my room, and because she's with me I don't fall to my knees and curl into a ball every few steps, the way I often do when no one is around. She nearly trips over my guitar that's been carelessly tossed in the corner. The heaviness of its presence feels like an albatross pulling me down. There have been times when I couldn't stand the sight of it. I've shoved it into closets, hid it under the bed, put it in the garage—always hoping its distance would allow me to forget I ever loved it.

I've been trying to un-hollow from the inside out and partying way too hard lately. Every spot from the Manhattan Bridge to Harlem is pulsing with a memory of Shay. The stairs at Lincoln Center. The park on 63rd. Our favorite Nolita bar. There is no escaping the traces of her.

Gwen picks up a photo booth picture I have lying on my end table. Shay and I had it taken the first night of our last tour. She drops it to the floor. "Have you spoken with her lately?"

I hurriedly pick it up and put it back on the end table. "If you consider stalking her on her social feeds talking to her, then yes, I speak to her every day." Her new blog, *Shots by Shay*, shines brightly with lush beaches, happy children, and all-around gorgeousness.

"Are you serious?" Gwen scrunches her face and cocks her head to the side.

"I miss her, but I have to limit how much we talk."

"You know my motto." She kicks some dirty clothes on the floor to the side.

"Enlighten me."

"You need to get under someone new to get over someone old."

"How do you stay so incredibly classy?" I rub my temples in disbelief.

"I'm just sayin'."

"Don't say that."

"What?"

"Don't say 'I'm just sayin'.' It annoys me when people say that."

"Why don't you come to a party with me tonight?"

"No, thank you."

"C'mon, it'll be fun. You remember fun, don't you?"

She hands me her phone and I read the party invite out loud: "*Vying Violette presents the Chantilly lace dance party at Chloe's 78.*"

"Neither a dance party nor a promoter named Vying Violette sound like my scene. Besides, I don't have anything to wear, and I'm not going shopping."

"You are more dramatic than a *Grey's Anatomy* storyline." She lets out an exasperated sigh. "First of all—"

"Yes, first of all, go on," I respond. Gwen knows I find it grating when she starts compiling lists as responses, and I think she does it on purpose.

"First of all, do you even know the type of people that will be at this party?" Gwen bites her thumb, hurls a flake of nail polish into the garbage bin, then starts on her left pointer finger.

"I am going to break out in a rash, you are so gross."

"Do you prefer I swallow my nail polish?"

"I prefer you take it off the typical way, you know, with remover."

"If it annoys you"—she shoves her nail deeper into her mouth—"it makes it that much more appealing." She makes a face like a rabbit as she scrapes her bottom row of teeth against her nail.

"And what type of people will be at this party?"

"People I think you will like."

I glance at her. "A person you like?" I say pointedly.

"I've been seeing someone for a few weeks." She smiles. "And maybe he'll be there tonight."

"Is it serious?"

"Well, we've shared a bed, or more aptly, a few nights, because the bed was the only place we didn't do it."

I roll my eyes. "Do I know him?"

"Uh, you might." Gwen averts her gaze.

For what feels like hours but ends up being merely minutes, Gwen carries on about every detail of her torrid love affair. She regales me with details of positions and places and what parts of his body look like, stopping just short of showing me photos. I feel very close to this enigmatic man, yet she guards the details that I actually need, such as what his fucking name is. This makes me slightly suspicious and extremely curious.

"Just come tonight and meet him," Gwen finishes. "You'll like him. He's like one of those extreme bicycle people."

"You mean motocross, you fucking grandmother?"

"Yeah, that."

"So, you want me to come and meet your next ex-boyfriend."

"Har, har, har." She makes a fake laughing snort.

My phone pings in my pocket.

It pings again. And again. And again.

I pull it out and collapse onto my bed. As if I'm in a horror film, about to open the door to a room I know I shouldn't go into, I look down at my phone. Shay's last post is of her smiling at the camera with a beautiful beach in the background. It's not the number of likes that climbs up every few second that bothers me—it's the woman with her arms around Shay's waist and her face nuzzled into Shay's neck.

My mouth opens and a shrill, manic scream releases from me.

"What?" Gwen stares at me. "What is it?"

I manipulate my frown into a calming smile.

"What is it?" She looks over my shoulder for my phone.

"It's Shay." I try not to react with full-blown panic. My shaky hand holds up my phone, and this spurs Gwen's excuses into action faster than if I was on fire. "Well, you don't know, they could be friends?"

"She put her on her social feed, Gwen." I give her the *give me a break* look. "Shay and I didn't even put ourselves on our feeds like this!" I claw my phone back and stare at the post, scrutinizing every angle, dissecting every detail.

"Shay put us into this strange position where we're both on some sort of adult gap year."

"May I make a suggestion?"

"What?" I lower my gaze.

"Come with me tonight." Her tone borders on begging.

"No."

"Please?" Now she's actually begging. Her eyes turn big and her lips press into a pout.

"The paparazzi are vultures. I don't want to deal with the exposure. I think our fans are beginning to realize that we were together and are now broken up."

"Yeah, there's no putting that genie back in the bottle. If your fans don't know, you should get smarter fans."

"You just have so many great jokes today. You should really consider taking this act on the road."

She smirks. "This is a private party. There's a list. And there's no way anyone will photograph you or write about you."

"You promise?"

"I promise." She flicks away another bit of nail polish and a tiny square of merlot red lands on my bed.

"Fine." I exhale dramatically.

She does a little victory dance. "Do you think you can wear something that's not so . . ." She pulls a T-shirt from my bed and holds it up. "Sophomoric?"

"Have at it." I point to the closet.

"Someone is going to mistake you for a fourteen-year-old boy." She drops the T-shirt onto the floor and leaves it there, then opens both closet doors in tandem.

"Don't you have an LBD?" she says into my clothes.

"A what?"

"Little Black Dress?"

"Yes, that's a hard pass."

Gwen's always been more stylish than me. She leaves the house in a way that looks incidental—a scarf here, smoky sunglasses there—but it's all engineered, labored over even. She always quotes that line by Dolly Parton: "It costs a lot of money to look this cheap."

My sister moves things back and forth until she pulls a black blazer from a hanger. She gets down on all fours and begins to rummage through shoes. She reaches behind the steamer trunk and tucked behind every pair of Vans and Adidas, she pulls out the only pair of heels I own. She's got a ball of clothes crumpled in her hands and the heels dangling from her fingers.

Gwen carefully lays out a pair of tight, ripped black jeans, a Blondie T-shirt, blazer, and the heels, also black. "This is how you show up. Trust me, you'll forget about Shay sooner rather than later."

"But I don't want to forget about her."

She holds the clothes up against me. "Admit it, this takes you to the next level."

"Ugh," I acquiesce, "fine." I grab the heels from her.

Gwen goes back to my closet and thumbs through the rest of my clothes, "Honestly, you should just burn all these Pause For Effect tees and start over." On more than one occasion Gwen's called my band's rise to fame "falling upward."

"Out." I point to the bedroom door. "Get out," I yell.

"I'm sorry, I'm sorry," Gwen laughs.

She sits down at my desk. "Why did you call me today then? What had you spiraling?"

"I was thinking about why I didn't go, and it hit me."

Gwen's eyes soften. "Why didn't you go with her?"

"She asked me if she was more important or the band. She positioned the two against each other, and it made me feel like I needed to make a choice." I pause, take a deep breath. "But I realize now that even though I had to make a choice, she never did. She left me here while she travels the world. She made the decision without even talking to me beforehand. Just asked me to join her, like a sad coda. She made me choose between two of the most important things to me, but never made the difficult choice herself. That's . . . that's why I stayed. That's why I'm still here."

Silence falls over us until finally, Gwen breaks it.

"You made the right call. Even if it doesn't feel that way." I nod.

"You need to learn how to exist by yourself and be happy by yourself. Without the band, without Shay, with just Taryn Taylor."

Her words hit me a little deep. The band and Shay have always been intertwined in my identity, and then they disappeared nearly simultaneously.

"This is why you shouldn't stop yourself from doing things for yourself. Come to the party tonight. Discover yourself. Fall in love with *you*." Gwen grins.

I laugh at her antics. "I think you're too thirsty for me to come. Despite my better judgment, I will take your sage advice, but this thirst feels suspicious."

She gets up for the door, but not before spitting one last bit of nail polish into my garbage bin. "All right, I'll be back for you tonight."

"Later," I sulk.

The afternoon slowly turns to evening, and my uneasiness starts to make butterflies jump around in my stomach. But I know Gwen is right. I don't know what is going on with Shay, other than we are apart, and I don't want to give Justin and Selena a run for their money in the on again/off again department. But this I know: being holed up inside my mother's house for the past few months has gotten me nowhere. A solid night out might not heal my heart's bruises, but it probably won't hurt them either.

• • •

The stranger to my right keeps eerily bumping his hand into mine on our shared subway pole, and the woman behind me is standing so incredibly close that I feel each exhalation of her warm breath steam down the back of my neck. NYC has no shortage of colorful people, and no matter where they're from, they all inevitably end up on the subway.

"Remind me again, why did we have to take the subway?" I glower at Gwen.

"Because I want you to remember what it's like to be around other humans."

"I am not taking the subway home later."

"We can get a car, that's fine."

The train comes to a jarring halt at the Bleecker Street station, pushing me dangerously close to Neck-breather, and my bag flies off my shoulder and down my arm. People lean back, bounce forward, and then do a dance when the subway doors fly open. I exhale in relief as I aggressively grab for Gwen, and we push our way out the door. We proceed up the stairs and turn right. When I get my bearings and figure out which exit to head for, I stumble upon two street performers deep into a melody. He's blowing into a baritone saxophone, and she's singing, shortening and lengthening different notes with each phrase. Hearing their music makes me ache inside—I desperately miss making music for people.

A crowd of at least twenty-five people has amassed, and every other person who walks up to them gives them a donation. The black banner that hangs behind them states their name and their purpose in glittering gold: *The Jazz Stylings of Matt & Gabbie*. A young man wearing a fedora sells codes to their digital download site off to the side. I hold out a twenty-dollar bill, and he hands me a card with a code and ten dollars' change. I throw the ten into the open saxophone case, which doubles as their donation jar, and stuff the card in between the pages of my journal.

We emerge from the underground into the cold air and walk down a snow-blanketed cobblestone street. Gwen leads me through a narrow alleyway and turns onto a dead-end street—not many of these in NYC. There's no signage outside Chloe's 78, and no online reviews. In fact, Gwen warned me that posting about my experience is highly discouraged. There's no address. You either know how to get there (through the kitchen of the bar next door), or you aren't invited.

"Gwen Taylor," Gwen tells the security guard manning the doorway. He looks down at his phone, scrolls, and then nods to let us in.

We make our way around the room. There are people dancing in the middle of the space, too drunk to care about how intertwined they are. The lights are low and the music is thumping loud enough for everyone to have to yell a little to hear each other. The smiling faces, the sweaty dancing, and the loud music feel a little out of place for me after months of eerie silence in my mom's living room, but it doesn't take long for me to feel the rhythm of the music flow through me. We settle at the L-shaped bar where Gwen cozies up to him—he's bald, bearded, and dark-skinned.

He introduces himself as "Bradley" as he unzips his hoodie, and when he pulls it off, Gwen pummels him with a hug.

I hold out my hand. "I'm Taryn, Gwen's sister. Pleasure to meet you."

He holds out his right hand and awkwardly shakes mine, his embrace of Gwen unwavering. "What are you having?" he offers.

"Whatever you're having."

"And you?" he asks Gwen.

She breaks off from him. "I'll have a club soda."

"You beg me to come out and you're not even drinking," I protest. "What the fuck?"

"A lady doesn't misbehave around a gentleman." She winks.

I shrug. I don't know what kind of role-playing shenanigan she's up to, but I also don't care all that much about whatever kink she's on tonight.

"One club soda, and she'll"—he points to me—"have a Miller High Life," he yells to the bartender.

The bartender cups his hand around his ear, the universal bartender sign for "say it again."

Bradley repeats the order.

I start my inquisition in a clear, sweet voice: "So you like my older sister."

Gwen steps on my foot.

Bradley feigns shock that Gwen's the older sister. "Very much so," he says wryly.

I look around the room. The crowd is just cool enough, not overdone, the music is just hip enough, nothing too obscure (yet), and the room is flowing, there's space between people, which is a rare find in the city.

"There's a DJ *and* a drummer. I'm not sure I've ever seen that combination before."

He snickers. "Can I tell you a secret?" He cocks his head.

"I've known you all of three minutes, but please do."

"I don't usually come to places like this, but Gwen told me she loves dance parties so I asked around, and a friend recommended any party Vying Violette puts on."

"Already doing her bidding?" I smirk but nudge him. "So . . . motocross rider?"

"Oh yeah. So . . . guitarist?"

"Yup." I beam. "Pause For Effect."

Bradley points at me. "Yes, yes, yes, I knew you looked familiar." He laughs.

"All kidding aside, your accent, I can't place it."

"Oh," he laughs again, "no one can. I was born here, lived in Germany until I was four. Then I moved to South Africa until I was a teenager, and in my twenties, I bounced all around Europe. I feel like every place I lived, I took a little bit of the accent with me." The corners of his mouth fill with excitement, and his eyes light up as he names every place he's lived.

"Why'd you move so much?"

"Army brat."

"Oh wow, who served, your mom or dad?"

He flinches when I mention his parents. "Dad." He nods but offers no other information. His mood shifts slightly. It's not hard to see there's a story there, but I glance at Gwen and decide not to press, not yet.

We clink our drinks to nothing in particular, perhaps other than wanting the painfully awkward moment to pass.

He goes on about motocross: catching air, his favorite bike, and the one trick he longs to master that will turn his sponsorship money into "fuck you" money.

He turns to Gwen and looks intently into her eyes. "I have to leave for a few weeks."

I snicker, wanting so badly to make a joke that Gwen's somehow pushed him away already, but one slicing glance from Gwen is all I need to know that I better not.

"But when I get back—I have a competition upstate—will you come watch me ride?" Bradley asks her.

She looks at me, searching for the answer.

"Yes, of course she will," I put in.

"You should come too, Taryn; bring your whole band."

"Well, what's left of it," Gwen immediately chimes in.

I elbow her in the ribs. Then I pull my phone out to look at the time and notice seven missed calls from an all-too-familiar number.

Gwen peers down at my phone. "Who is that?"

"It's Sofia fucking Alexi, and she's a vulture."

"Is that her full name: Sofia Fucking Alexi?"

"Honestly," I take a sip of my drink, "it should be."

"Why is she calling you so much?"

"I don't know," I flip my phone over, "and I don't care."

Gwen pulls it off the bar. "She left you a voicemail." She waves the phone in the air.

I take it back, plug one ear, and play the voicemail. I can barely make out what she's saying. I squint my eyes as if it'll help me make out the words any clearer.

"She's doing a top ten list of Pause For Effect's favorite songs, ranked in order by us, and wants my input."

The bartender hands Gwen another club soda. She clinks her glass with me and then Bradley. "That's fun, right?"

"No, she's needling me, Gwen." I put my phone down. "Parker probably replied immediately to suck the blood out of any mention of him in the press. She knows Shay is out of the country and probably hasn't responded. And Nelson is probably avoiding her, too. I'm sure she just wants to get me to give a quote about Parker's solo success."

"Wow," Bradley exclaims. "You deduced all of that through a voicemail you could barely hear?"

"Trust me." I take a final swig of my beer and put it back down on the bar. "When you live in a space where pseudo-journalists are always trying to get your attention, you pick up an honorary degree in identifying their tactics."

Bradley responds to me, but I can no longer focus on what he's saying. I've fallen victim to the beautiful woman across the bar whose fierce stare borders on rude. I watch as she meticulously reapplies her red lipstick. I slowly walk across the bar right toward her, only to be interrupted by Gwen. "Here, take your bag." She shoves it in my hand, looking over in the direction of the woman. "I have a feeling you won't be coming back."

I feel the vibrations of the blaring music, and I know people are singing along because their mouths are moving. Time slows down. The air becomes still. And I lean in to introduce myself to her, imposing slightly on her personal space. "Hi, I'm Taryn Taylor."

"I am Violette. Violette Dufresne. Nice to meet you, *Tah-rin.*" Violette looks at me in wonderment.

"I know you."

"You do?" She sounds genuinely shocked.

"From the party flyer." My smile lingers for more than a beat. "Do you live here, in the city?"

"*Ah non*, I am only here for a month, promoting this party. Paris is my home."

Her eyes are deep, dark, and dangerous. Her French lilt is thick, and her eyelashes are thicker.

Violette raises her glass, swallows hard, and laughs a little.

I could get used to hearing that laugh.

"I know you, actually." She cocks her head a bit. "Aren't you," she pauses, "in that band . . . ?"

"Pause For—" I start.

"Oh, yes. Effect." She finishes my sentence. "Parker." She pronounces it *Parr-kurr*. She flashes an inviting million-dollar smile. "Yes, of course, I just heard his new song."

I want to scream.

"How is it, playing without him?" She opens her eyes wide and tilts her head in a come-hither fashion.

"Well, we're actually on hiatus right now—"

"Too bad." She emphasizes *bad* as she leans forward, moving her sumptuous body closer to mine. "Your music is cool." Which she pronounces like, *koo-le*.

I smirk, unsure of where the French hold compliments like *cool* in their vernacular. I don't bother to respond, instead, just assault her with question after question about her life. She seems to know me, and I'd like to know her better.

She regales me with stories about parties she's recently thrown in Belize, or did she say Maldives? And that her favorite spots to throw parties require you to go off the grid for a week at a clip. And last year, at one of her biggest bashes, she turned down the famous director Robert Reatnay, because the same night she met supermodel Stella and started dating her instead.

"I am throwing a party in Paris that you must come to, *chérie*." She stares deeply at me. "You will love it."

"And how exactly do you know what I will love?" I lower my gaze.

"Dark, sultry lounge, burlesque dancers . . . The ambience will make you blush." She caresses my cheek with her hand.

It turns out, she does know what I will love.

A freshly shaven railing of a man rushes over to Violette. An assistant, maybe. He hands her a glass of red wine and then whispers in her left ear. She looks disinterested in his disruption, disappointed even.

"I am afraid I must go." Violette hands me a thick-stock card dipped in the most intense purple, with the words

Vying Violette on the front and a brief description on the back:

Violette Dufresne
"C'est toujours le bon moment"
@VyingViolette

I attempt to say *"C'est toujours le bon moment"* in French.

"It's always the right time," Violette translates.

I repeat, *"C'est toujours le bon moment,"* conscious that I might be flirting with her. Noting how easily it comes to me.

"See, you can speak French." She takes one swallow and leaves her nearly full wine glass on the bar.

"I'll jot it down in my notebook next to the two German phrases I know: 'Let me roll that blunt for you' and 'Guns and children are welcome.' "

She looks at me curiously. "You are very funny." She runs one finger under my chin. Then lowers her voice to a whisper and leans in toward me. "I am going back to France in six weeks. Call me soon."

My cheeks burn and my insides swirl.

I open my bag to do something I will undoubtedly regret. I put her business card inside the pages of my journal. Promising myself that when I return to find her number, I will deal with the contents of this leather-bound hindrance. I risk another glance in Violette's direction. She looks back over her shoulder at me and smiles.

Am I betraying Shay by accepting another woman's phone number? I want Shay to be happy, I do. But mostly,

I want permission to call Violette. Or at least, I need for Shay to forgive me when I do.

I turn on my heel and see Gwen motioning for me to come back over to her. "I just got us a car," she tells me when I approach.

"A car already?"

"Yeah." She yawns. "I'm bone-tired today, I can't shake it."

"Well, should we take two cars? Aren't you going back to your place?"

"Nah, I'll come to Mom's, we can have a sleepover."

"Should we say goodbye to Bradley?" I look around for him.

She shakes her head. "He went to the bathroom, and I want to take off while he's in there. Leave him wanting more."

"It comes as no surprise to me that you're perpetually single."

She looks down at a blinking notification on her phone. "C'mon, our car's here. Let's go before he sees us leaving."

It's started to snow, and we barely make it into our on-demand chariot unscathed. Our driver's BMW 325i reeks of men's cologne and bleach. He shifts from fourth to fifth gear and weaves in and out of lanes in a way that makes me wonder whether I'll make it to my next birthday. I see every tree, curb, and side mirror come toward me at full speed. Every random rock and piece of earth that we run over sounds like its velocity will send it right through the tan leather seats. The little alcohol I had is lurching in my stomach.

"Sir," I lean up to the front seat a little, "can you drive a little slower?"

He grunts and eases up on the accelerator.

"Thank you, sir."

I hear a familiar song playing on the radio. "Sir, can you turn that song down a little?" I ask.

"Hey, it's your little band playing on the radio," Gwen interjects.

"Gwen, you are such an ass. You love my *little* band when it's benefitting you. Like, oh yeah, when I introduce you to famous people, and then you get gigs doing their makeup."

She rummages through her bag, looking for her phone. "You know what, you're right, and while I'm thanking you: thanks for coming tonight." She takes her phone out and pulls up Bradley's social feed. "Look at how hot he is!"

I give Gwen the *here we go* eyebrow raise.

She laughs.

"So what's his deal?"

"His deal?"

"Yeah, his deal? Where did he grow up? Where do his parents live? Is there generational wealth? Where does his family summer? You know, his deal."

"Oh, well, he lost both of his parents in separate car accidents. I believe they were middle class, the Collins, so no generational wealth, and therefore he doesn't summer anywhere but he sees lots of countries with riding so, he's like, very well-rounded and worldly."

That she spent more time breaking down his wealth than his parent's death is unsettling. "That's why he flinched when he mentioned his dad."

"You asked about them?" She guffaws.

"No, not on purpose, it just came up. Shit, I didn't know; you should've warned a bitch not to say anything."

"Yeah, he doesn't like to talk about him—like, at all—his dad was cheating on his mom, and his mom followed him out late one night. The woman his dad was having the affair with was drunk, ran a stop sign, and they all crashed: his dad and the mistress in one car, and his mom in the other."

"You couldn't even write a tragedy like that. That's borderline fiction."

"I know." She shakes her head. "It's so heartbreaking."

I stare out the window, not sure how to process Bradley's story. It's the type of thing songs are written about, movies are made about, books are based on.

"I suppose it makes your problems seem tiny by comparison," Gwen muses.

"Huh," I look back at her, "my problems?"

"Yeah, Shay, and your focus on your path forward."

"What?" the driver asks, assuming that Gwen is speaking to him.

"Not you," she says, leaning forward.

"Focus on what makes you happy," she tells me.

"Shay made me happy." I stare back out the window at the dark night. "She's gone. My band made me happy, and I'm not sure, but it may very well be gone too." I shake my head.

"Do you mean to tell me that my overachieving little sister—the one who defied all odds and became famous just out of high school—can't get her life together enough to come out on top?"

"You might be right. I might need to *come on top*."

"I said come out on top."

"I know, I'm making a joke."

"You should work on your material." She snorts.

"Gwen, am I a horrible person if I sleep with Violette?"

She crinkles her nose when she smiles hard. "I'm so proud of you right now."

"Sir, you passed our house, it's just behind us on the right," I tell the driver. "Yeah, right there." I point.

The driver turns around and looks at the both of us. "This house right here?" He points at Mr. Kelsey's house.

"Yes," we say at the same time.

We laugh like schoolchildren as he pulls out of Mr. Kelsey's driveway and we traipse across his yard. When we see his front porch light turn on, we book it.

Chapter 8
Devil May Care

Adults gather to admire the flickering, dazzling luminosities with a fascination typically exhibited by children. It happens every Christmas season on Fifth Avenue. In this obstinate maze of holiday window-shopping scenes, people are teeming with gift-buying purpose, whether they're going against the stream of the crowd in Times Square or with the flow to see the tree at 30 Rock.

A little over a month ago, I dug deep into the pages of my journal to find Violette's phone number. Her card was stuck against the download code for Matt & Gabbie's album.

We've been on more than the requisite three dates since we first met, so as far as the rules of dating go, we can now sleep together.

It's 11 p.m. By New York City standards, it's early. On the way to the restaurant, as I cross over Sixth Avenue, I come across several characters behaving as if they've just escaped a home for the unhinged: "Go fuck yourself, George," one calls out to himself, and his two companions just look on with creased faces, as if agreeing that George should indeed go fuck himself.

I push open the door to La Maison de Magdalena and wait by the hostess stand. A man standing next to me, also waiting for the hostess to return, comments on a woman in a black trench coat who just breezed past us, interrupting my reverie. "We live in New York City. A gal's stilettos might as well cost as much as a car. They probably get more miles," he says in the most dad-joke kind of way.

I look down at the woman's heels, and then my gaze travels up her back to her pin-straight black hair. Violette isn't inconvenienced by idle waiting—she's being seated by the first waiter who laid eyes on her. He seats her at a corner table, pulling the seat facing outward so that she has a view of the entire restaurant. He hangs her coat, gloves, and scarf in the coat check. She looks like she belongs to the city of Paris, but I want her to belong to me, if only for tonight.

Once she's seated, she notices me and we lock eyes. I walk over to her. By contrast, I pull out my own seat, the one offering a view only of Violette. I place my coat on the back of my chair and shove my gloves into my coat pockets.

I look around. The place has a faux-French vibe to it. I would imagine this type of imitation to be grating to someone who spends most of their time in actual French brasseries in Paris. I conclude my once-over of the place and smile at her.

I want to ask her if we can ditch the niceties and go back to her hotel.

She breaks the ice. "Do you eat oysters?"

"Yes." I consciously control my breathing. My nerves churn as I suddenly realize that I have no idea how to start a conversation that ultimately leads to sex. I've spent most of my adult life in love with Shay. *Fuck, please, no, don't think of Shay now.*

The waiter comes over, providing a brief pardon for my racing thoughts.

"We will have two dozen bluepoint oysters," Violette tells the very tall waiter, who is bending over to take our order.

She leans in. "If we were in Paris, I would have ordered you the Gillardeau, but I must make do with what they serve here." She shrugs.

"When are you going back?"

"I am returning tomorrow."

"Tomorrow?" I stammer.

"*Oui.* You will come sometime, *oui?*"

"I think so, *oui.*" I know the invitation is superficial, as is my commitment to going, but it's what you do when someone invites you to their place in Paris—you tell them, "Yes, of course, next time I'm in France I'll look you up."

My right knee bounces up and down despite my private warning to myself to stop it. I want to impress this woman, and she is a woman, in age and in attitude. The waiter has been patiently hovering over me for more than a beat, and I realize he's waiting to take my drink order. Painfully aware of how out of place I suddenly feel, I order what I believe is the best bottle of wine on the menu: "And we'll have a bottle of the 2016 Château Figeac, St-Émilion Grand Cru."

He takes both of our wine glasses from the table with him as he walks away. He returns several minutes later with two fresh new glasses and a bottle. He shows it to me and I nod. He pours an eighth of a glass and waits for me to try it.

"It's delicious."

He pours us each a glass.

Her soft, full lips push up against the glass as she takes a delicate sip; it troubles me how envious I am of an inanimate object.

She places the glass down and smooths her napkin on her lap. "Your band," she begins, "is over?"

I smile outwardly, but inwardly I'm flattened. A moment ago, I was hanging from the monkey bars, but someone came along and pushed me down, and now I'm facedown, flat on my stomach in the sandbox. The air has been sucked out of me, but I have to keep my eyes wide open and answer her.

"I certainly hope not." I grin.

"A band with a devil-may-care attitude like yours is always easy to find again." Violette closes her eyes and raises the tips of her index fingers to her eyelids, which are dusted with the most subtle shade of black. Then she opens her eyes and stares back at me.

"Devil may care," I repeat to her. If ever there were a phrase to sum up who she is, it just came falling out of her mouth—and she used it to describe Pause For Effect.

"We definitely need a new singer." I rub my fingers up and down the stem of my wine glass.

"Have you been looking?"

"Nelson and I have, but our effort to find the right singer has been infuriating."

"Oh?" She seems intrigued. "How so?"

"Simply put, in the two-minute movie montage version, our attempts would fall somewhere between comic relief and pitifully sad. Finding a qualified singer that Nelson and I vibe with is an exhausting endeavor." I gesture as if he were sitting with us at the table. "I put out an ad, filter through responses, hold rehearsals—and singers ghost us."

She laughs the most adorable laugh. It motivates me to go on. Leaning in: "There was the one guy who missed too many band practices. There was the woman who was an incredible singer. She didn't come right out and say she was in trouble with the law, but she also didn't have to—after several rehearsals, and several hundred excuses, it became obvious. Then there was the aging rocker who constantly insulted our sound and the direction we wanted to go in, and we had to suffer through the barrage of war stories of musicians he's played with, roadie gigs he's had. I basically threw him out of the rehearsal studio when he went on a tear about groupies he's fucked (his words, absolutely not mine). And don't get me started on the talentless hacks who would show up to meet us simply because we were the founding members of the band Parker used to be in. Lather, rinse, repeat."

"And what about Shay—does she not have a say in who joins the band?"

And what about Shay . . .

The waiter's appearance with our oysters can only be described as right on cue.

I rub my left temple. "It's all in shambles." He lights a candle and sets it in the middle of the table. "And Shay's in, I think, South America?" I shrug my shoulders, uncomfortable discussing Shay with Violette.

The ambient light offers me the chance to stare at Violette outright. I catalog the beauty of her pale skin contrasted against her bright red lipstick. She is clearly at least ten years my senior. The tiny lines around her eyes, the ones that make her expressions more dramatic, reveal this more than any online search about her age ever could.

"Oh, it sounds very," she takes a slurp of an oyster, "dramatic."

"Slightly." I look down. "Well, not dramatic, just not really the details an artist cares to concern herself with. I just want to make music, and nothing is more depressing than the business of making music."

I pick up an oyster and slug it down, noting how absolutely graceless this act is.

"Maybe, with half the band being on hiatus, you should start a new one, *non?*"

I laugh to hide my disappointment. And contrary to every instinct, I blurt something out of left field, changing the topic from something that makes me feel shattered and exposed to something that will perhaps make her feel the same. "Hey, are you still dating Stella?" The internet is good for nothing if not learning about someone's lover.

I take a swig of wine and wait to see if I've just supremely fucked up an opportunity to go home with Violette Dufresne.

"No." She shrugs and looks out into the middle of the restaurant for a moment. "To be honest, it feels like it's been years since I've connected with someone in a real way. You see, I date people in the spotlight, and that comes with"—she stops to search for the words—"well, you know all about dating famous people, right?"

"Are you referring to me and Shay?" I eloquently surmise.

"You both did a good job keeping it from the public." She laughs as she shakes her head left to right.

"Well, not so good if the news made it all the way to France?" My hand lands on the table, outstretched toward her.

"I guess, *oui*. But my publicist told me when I said I had a few dinners with you. You can't hide anything from a publicist." She puts her hand on the table, outstretched toward mine on the other side of the table. "But to the public—I am saying this as a member of the public— you've done a supremely good job of hiding it."

"We aren't really hiding it."

"Are not," she cocks her head, "or were not?"

"I should probably correct my tenses." I look into my glass, then up again to smile at her. "We *were* not." I am very conscious that my attempt at flirting while discussing my ex-girlfriend borders on offensive, even to me, and I'm the one trying to pull it off.

One bottle of wine turns into two, and before you know it, the waiter is handing us a tiny clipboard which houses the bill. He places it in the middle of the table and we wrestle over it. Not in a polite pull-and-tug either—neither of us will relent. I stand up to pull my coat off the back of my chair, and this movement distracts Violette just long enough for me to grab the bill holder from her grip. I beam, proud that I am able to take it from her. I affix my card to the clipboard and swing my arm over the table to hand it to the waiter, who is patiently and idly standing by. As the bill holder reaches his hand, my arm stiffens and my face turns to stone as I note that the candle has made the arm of my jacket catch fire.

"*Au feu!*" Violette yells as she jumps up from the table.

"*Fire!*" The waiter calls out.

I struggle to rip my coat off, and when the sleeve hits the table, the tablecloth, too, catches fire.

Patrons dart to the front of the restaurant. Seats are left abandoned. A busboy comes running from the back, fire extinguisher in hand, and in one swift movement, he pulls the pin out and douses me, the coat, and the table. White speckles fill the air like New Year's Eve confetti and a heavy chemical scent wafts through the room. The sixty-second ordeal feels like a lifetime.

And that's when the sprinklers come on, drenching us all.

The restaurant swells with competitive guffaws from those who remain inside. I hang my coat over my left arm.

It looks as if I painted my apartment white while wearing it. I make a huge deal out of saying sorry to every person within my eyeline. The waiter walks back to Violette, who has a small smile on her face as she watches me apologize countless times, and he places her trench coat over her shoulders, then hands her her scarf and gloves. Violette walks away, giggling a little, and my gaze follows the course of her stilettos as they click through the restaurant. We hear the fire truck sirens wail as we walk down the street, and without a hint of irony, she lights a cigarette. She nourishes my eyes but leaves me ravenous with hunger at the same time. The only way to satiate my appetite will be to devour her whole.

• • •

Soaking wet and with a half-charred coat is how I end up at Violette's hotel. All eyes shift to her as she walks across the lobby. You can tell by her swagger that this is a familiar occurrence when she walks through any room.

"Miss Dufresne!" the concierge calls across the lobby. "I have a package for you." He waves her over and hands her an envelope.

She puts her hand on top of his and thanks him.

"You're wet," he says to her.

Much like Gwen, I want to hide my face in my armpit and laugh at his innocent observation that I've turned into an indecent remark.

"Yes, the sprinklers went off," Violette says, pointing up to the twenty-foot ceiling.

His glance shifts between the two of us. Violette looks well put together and her coat hides most of the damage the water caused. Her makeup has held, and her hair has since stopped dripping. By contrast, I look like I was dipped in glue and steamrolled over Fifth Avenue after the Pride parade.

The elevator whizzes and soars to our destination on the twenty-eighth floor.

She opens the door to the penthouse suite and points to a mat on the floor. I place my water-logged coat and shoes on it and put my bag off to the side. I cannot discern whether I'm here to seduce her or she just feels badly for me.

I walk deeper into the room, drawn to the floor-to-ceiling windows. From our vantage point, the surrounding buildings have an anonymous yet familiar feel to them. It's as if I am seeing the bird's-eye view shot during the opening credits of a film set in the West Village.

Our glances become more frequent and tense. The way her body moves toward me makes me want to teach her things she never thought she needed to learn. My stomach muscles vacillate between butterflies and knots. I am close enough to smell both the sweet scent of wine and the sordid scent of cigarettes on her breath. We press our bodies tightly against each other and I hold her face in my hands. And all at once, it becomes painfully obvious that the residual chemical smell of the fire extinguisher is too distracting for us to continue.

"Is it too forward to offer you the shower?" Her seductive gaze is trained on me.

"I don't think it is." I look down at the state I'm in. She's right. It also would've been well within her rights not to invite me over at all.

She throws her hair into an elaborate twist and wraps a band around it once, twice. "Well, it's just over there . . ." She wraps the band around her bun a third time and points to the hallway. "Third door on the left."

As I'm walking toward the door, I turn back around. "Oh." I peel my shirt slightly away from my stomach to illustrate its damp status. "I don't have anything to change into."

Her smoky, seductive voice sighs, "You won't need clothes."

It takes me some time to bring myself to strip off my clothes entirely. The situation is proving itself more difficult than I expected—both removing the wet clothes and coaxing myself to accept that my actions will have consequences.

I hear Nelson's voice in my head, something he said when Shay and I first started dating. "When it comes to shitting where you eat—you are somewhat of a prodigy." And now I am about to sleep with a woman when I am in love with another woman.

I run my hands along the slate stone tiling the walls and floor. It's cool and gives off an outdoor vibe, like showering in the wild. I turn the faucets. Water rushes at me from the ceiling and three of the walls that surround me. I have friends with studio apartments smaller than this shower.

My mind races with competing thoughts—Violette's voice, soft and authoritative: "You won't need clothes"— abruptly interrupted by thoughts of Shay. Her soft olive skin and smiling face flash before my eyes. It feels as though I am betraying her, even though I haven't seen her in months. By all accounts, Violette is a stranger, and tonight, no matter how sumptuous or desired, is going to get me into trouble. The madness in my mind slowly overcomes me, and I find myself crouching on the floor of the shower.

Despite being in a beautiful French woman's shower, edging dangerously close to two in the morning, I resolve to keep the friendship platonic. I stand and straighten myself up, bolstered by a new agenda to steer this ship back to neutral territory—maybe a conversation about our childhood or our families. I could always use a party promoter friend in France. And if I bore her with stories of my dead father, I'm sure to turn her off.

Violette knocks, and without waiting for me to respond, enters, wearing nothing but a pair of black lace panties.

She surreptitiously lets her hair out of its bun. Her black lace panties drop to the ground, and the pit in my gut drops too.

"Come with me." She pulls me out of the shower.

"Yes," I nod, intoxicated. I am entirely at her mercy.

She hands me a towel and I modestly put it around me.

She walks me into the bedroom and I drop the towel to the floor. She's confident but slightly reserved, and then loses some of herself when she pulls her body closer to mine. I press my lips against hers. Her eyes are soft and affectionately fixed upon me. She lays herself down on the king bed and I get on top of her and run my hand up her thigh.

• • •

In bed, our intertwined bodies lie naked for hours, refusing to let our embrace relent, even as we drift in and out of sleep. We oscillate between lovemaking and slumber. All I can see behind her somewhat sheer blinds are the twinkling lights of the cityscape, making her look all the more surreal.

In that sweet spot between the ending of a late night and the start of an early day, the dark dissolves around us. When the sun slowly creeps out from behind the neighboring buildings, I quietly crawl out of bed and slip down the hallway to put on my half-dry clothes. I look for a pen to leave her a note but can't find one. Instead, I slink out of her hotel room, and when I exit the lobby, I look left and then right. I know where I must go next, and as if on autopilot, I head there.

Chapter 9

Everything Is
Hotsy-Totsy Now

Going from Violette's hotel room back to my mom's felt weird. Like taking-a-shower-with-your-shoes-on weird. I stumble upon a woman in her early twenties sitting on the curb near the coffee shop. She yells, "Change!" at me. I throw some in her bucket and tell her, "Change is inevitable."

Nelson's agreed to meet me. I am, after all, in his neighborhood.

"Black coffee with skim milk for Terry," the barista calls as he looks around for the drink's soon-to-be owner.

"It's Taryn!" I say, annoyed. I don't know why I bother giving my real name anymore. Without fail, baristas always get it wrong. Tara, Tanya, Tola—once, some teen-ager called out "Tarzan, black drip for Tarzan."

The music pumps loudly through the coffee shop, the notes pulsing across the room before dissipating into the air. I secure us a table, and when I decide it is not private enough, I snag another one.

"What are you wearing?" He asks in a petulant tone.

"It's a long story and one I don't feel like getting into right this second."

He shrugs, consults his phone, sending what looks like an important text and stares impatiently at the screen as he awaits a reply.

"Everything all right over there—in your phone?"

"Huh? Oh, yes." He puts his phone down and looks back up at me.

The music fades out from the ceiling and a familiar radio DJ's voice floats through the air: ". . . he's been named one of the most desirable pop singers . . ."

Parker's most recent hit, "Divide," plays out.

I point to the speaker that hangs on the wall as if a tiny version of Parker is inside it, crooning.

A bystander waiting for her coffee turns into our corner and gives Nelson a sidelong glance. "You look exactly like your sister."

I stand up, instinctively coming between the woman and Nelson like I'm breaking up a fight. "Sofia Alexi," I scowl. I would recognize her witch-like brown eyes and coal-black hair anywhere. My hatred for this woman runs deep.

"Oh, it's like a two-for-one!" She shakes her shoulders like a two-year old dances. "It's fifty percent of Pause For Effect. I might as well just sit down here and do an interview."

"No thank you," Nelson and I say in tandem, and it's Nelson who continues: "You can get an interview the same way everyone else can—through our agent."

"That's too bad." A Cheshire cat grin spans across her face. "We're doing an exclusive with Parker, and it would've been fun to have his *old* band's perspective to round out the interview."

The way she says "his old band" is all tragedy and no comedy.

"Why don't you just stick to interviews with DJs who spell their name with a lot of *Z*'s at the end and forget about Pause For Effect?"

"Oh, Taryn, sweetie, if you keep turning down interviews and Parker's success continues to eclipse yours, me and the rest of the world will forget about Pause For Effect."

I'm in ready-to-pounce mode. "Do you actually consider yourself a journalist? You're a hack! Do you think the world needs more articles about celebrity pregnancies? Or in-depth articles about how lemon can *totes* save your stained shirt. Or listicles of ten writers who became famous after they died." I roll my eyes.

"Speaking of far more famous after death than when they were alive—I'm doing an entire series deconstructing the song lyrics of Timothy Taylor and the Standards."

"What is your obsession with me, Sofia?"

"With you personally? Actually, nothing. But as you very well know, the people around you are pretty interesting."

The barista calls out Sofia's coffee order, and she picks it up from the counter.

"Well, this has been fun." She waves as she walks out the door. "Toodles, Taryn."

"I cannot fucking stand Sofia Alexi!" I yell out way louder than I intend to.

"I know." Nelson puts his hand on my back and motions for me to take a seat. "Simmer down." His deep voice is soothing, but I still feel the rage bubbling.

"She thinks my band will be forgotten. Ha! Yeah, okay, Sofia Alexi. You'll see, Sofia Alexi, my band's comeback is going to be bigger than Britney Spears."

"Taryn," Nelson interrupts me, "she's left."

But I keep on going. "Parker, he will come back. It'll be nostalgic, like Justin Timberlake going back to *NSYNC."

"You are bending my ear."

"Our comeback is going to be bigger than Jesus'!"

"I don't mean to get cross, but Taryn, you are yelling."

"And then she brings my father into it." I guffaw.

He slices me with his gaze, the one that implies that I need to stop talking so loudly, and I finally take a deep breath, trying to reset myself to calm.

His phone goes off again and I hear the ping, ping, ping ringing out from his pocket.

"It's an email from Four Chords. Parker's new video for 'Divide' is out." He flashes his phone screen at me. "Do we watch it?"

"Oh, whatever," I scoff. "This day already sucks ass, and we're gonna see it eventually. No better time than now."

I would never admit this to Nelson, but I desperately want to see the video. As uncomfortable as it'll make me to suffer through it, a part of me needs to judge him—and another needs to see the comments section firsthand, to witness how well received is his newfound glory without us.

"Maybe it'll suck," Nelson says as he presses the sideways triangle icon on his phone.

The scene opens on what looks like an exact replica of Pause For Effect onstage. The spikes in Parker's hair have been lopped and replaced with a tame forward swoop. He's even dyed it an expensive shade of honey brown—his most significant change in hairstyle since I've known him. He's wearing glasses and looks directly into the camera lens, sullen and serious. I know every one of Parker's manufactured looks and what they mean, and worst of all, where they lead. The "band" behind him in the video looks absurdly styled, like model/actor versions of me, Shay, and Nelson. The camera zooms in on Parker, his face all scrunched up in make-believe agony as he scream-sings the words: "You caused the divideeeeeeeee!"

And then they cut to an elevator scene. All three of our doppelgängers plus the real Parker, played by himself, are stuck in it. I know this scene because I lived through it. Parker's song is a thinly veiled reference to me and Shay, which didn't even occur to me until this moment, as I watch the visual accompaniment.

"This! Is! Our! Band!" I yell at Nelson. "Let me guess, the singer is going to light a cigarette next and the elevator gets stuck!"

Nelson smirks and points down at the phone when my prediction comes true. I glare at Nelson, then back at his phone screen.

And then it happens.

I've never been slapped across the face, but this must be what it feels like, this flushed heat, this stinging pain in my cheeks.

Faux-Shay is pulling faux-Taryn in close, they're making out with each other against a wall.

"This is the worst video," Nelson announces. "Do we even press on?"

"Keep it on," I demand. "I cannot fucking believe this!"

The video comes to an end. The bassist and guitarist stand, holding hands, a heart icon closes in on them, and the end credits roll up with the words "Let's show our pride by donating to change.org."

Nelson's eyes have a spark to them. He is patient about everything except for people fucking with his sister.

My eyes are moist. "He outed us, and we're no longer a couple." The irony borders on cruel. It was not his right to do this. It was our personal journey to come out to our fans in our own way, like we wanted to, when we were ready. It feels so heartbreaking to have something so personal and intimate shared without our consent.

"I can't believe Bill Sweeney allowed this." Nelson furrows his brow.

My phone explodes with @ mentions and pings from all over the Twitterverse, and I snatch it up from the table. I look up at Nelson, who's craning his neck up as if mulling over my suggestion.

"You should call Shay."

"No." I shake my head.

"Taryn." Nelson grins. "You should."

"There's a reason I called you this morning. There's a reason why I'm in your neighborhood so early."

"Well, go on. You can tell me anything."

I take a deep breath. Nelson can get lost in a parking lot while using a GPS, yet when it comes to knowing that I'm doing someone I probably shouldn't be doing, his instincts are impeccable.

"Spill it."

I don't do anything. I don't say anything. I simply stare at him.

"Who is she?"

"A party promoter. Vying Violette. She doesn't even live here; she's from France."

"How long have you been seeing her?"

"About a month. She's going back to Paris tonight."

"You can dally with strangers, but what about my sister . . ." he whispers.

"Shay is seeing someone!"

"You are so daft." He raises an eyebrow. "You didn't go with her. You barely even talk to her."

"But—" I gasp. "She's the one who left me!"

Bonnie Tyler's "Total Eclipse of the Heart" rings out from Nelson's pocket. He sheepishly glances down at his phone. "Well, speak of the devil."

My hands are shaking as he hands me his phone, and every emotion comes flooding back as if she'd never left. "Hi," I pause. "Shay."

Chapter 10
Honest and Truly

I've fantasized for months now about how to start a conversation with Shay that goes beyond stalking her blog and adding likes and comments to her social feed. I so badly want to execute the perfect balance of wit and sexiness. So as I raise Nelson's phone to my ear and open my mouth, I don't expect to hang up on her—but I do.

"Oh my god, that cyclist! He just got hit by a car," I yell out to Nelson, jumping up and motioning to the person sprawled out on the sidewalk. I throw him his phone and he runs out. I watch the cyclist getting help from passersby and Nelson. Then I pick up my phone and go to my favorites—her number is still first on the list. I tap the call icon.

This is not how I expected my first real conversation with Shay to start.

She picks up at once.

"I am so sorry," I sigh. "A cyclist just got hit by a car."

"Oh, wow."

"I know."

"Well, do you have to go then?" she asks. Her tone sounds as if she expects me to hang up again.

"No—" I look out the window at Nelson moving the bike closer to the coffee shop and the driver of the car helping the guy up onto the sidewalk. "I was momentarily derailed, but I'm all yours now." I sit back down in my seat, still keeping an eye on the window. "Did you see the video?" My words make me stand right back up again and start to pace the coffee shop, much to the annoyance of some customers that I don't really care about right now.

"Yeah, I'm still on the Four Chords distro list. They sent out a promo email about an hour ago."

Her voice tears a hole through my chest. I miss her accent. I miss her diction. I miss everything about her.

"Is it late? What time zone are you in?" I ask.

"Time zone? Is that really what you want to focus on?"

"I'm not sure." I exhale loudly. "I don't really have a roadmap for how to handle this conversation. I feel like it's a borderline business meeting and my wires are getting all crossed."

"I can't believe that when we finally talk, it's about Parker." She sounds frustrated.

"It's always about Parker." I laugh.

Shay takes on an unfamiliar tone. "Yeah, not for me. Not anymore."

"Can we not do this over the phone?" I say, exasperated.

"Well, to answer your question, I'm in a time zone just an hour ahead of you."

"I haven't seen you post in a few days."

"I'm in São Paulo."

"How's it all going?"

"It's honestly been life-altering."

"Shit, that sounds pretty dramatic."

"It is, actually."

"Well, tell me, I want to know . . ."

"I don't really want to get into it right now." She still sounds a little impatient.

"I guess I'm just going to have to wait."

"Well," she says, "you aren't going to have to wait much longer."

"What do you mean?"

"I'm coming back, Taryn." Her confession quiets my mind.

"You're coming," I stutter, "home? When? For Christmas?"

"No, I'll miss the holidays. I'll be back next month."

Continuing to pace, I open the side door to the coffee shop and slip through it. Nelson is sitting against the brick side of the coffee shop with the cyclist, talking to him. I wave at him from a distance and start walking down the street. I'm sure he'll start furiously texting me any minute asking where I am off to.

"Why are you coming home early?" I ask Shay calmly, trying not to convey the hope in my voice.

"It's been an amazing run, but after I launched my blog, *Shots by Shay*, a gallery owner called, and I'm doing an entire exhibition."

"Holy shit, where?" Try as I might to keep myself together and sound nonchalant, excitement radiates through my voice.

"The Lower East Side."

"Holy fuck. NYC." I exhale a sign of relief. "That's incredible."

"Yeah."

Even over the phone, I can tell she's smiling. Finally.

I take a long pause and stare at a plastic grocery bag stuck in the branches of a sidewalk tree, contemplating where to take the conversation. My reverie is broken by a deluge of texts from Nelson:

Where are you going?

Are you on the phone with Shay?

The EMTs just loaded the guy into an ambulance. That was crazy.

Come back to the coffee shop.

He was fine, btw.

Taryn?

"I can't believe he did that to us." Shay's voice is filled with anger again.

"Yes!" I reply. It feels validating to have Shay on my side again. "I still haven't processed it properly. But I know I'm angry. He shouldn't have done this without telling us."

"I want to talk to him in person, but I don't even know if I want to *see* him." Shay's tone shifts from angry to conflicted.

I stare up at the traffic light as it's changing from red to green and wait for the walk sign. The silence between us causes me to just spill out the question that's been bubbling inside me.

"Are you dating her?" I ask accusingly.

"I miss your direct, bordering-on-rude tone."

"Oh, I certainly don't mean to be rude."

"It's fine. I know you don't mean to be. Yes, I was dating her."

"Was? That's promising." My voice betrays the sound of hope shining through.

"Taryn, with every iota of love for you I can muster, I don't want to talk about this right now."

"Right, okay, sorry."

"Damn it, Taryn. It's been nearly five months, and Parker—Parker is the reason we get on the phone?" She brings it up again, still sounding as frustrated as before, even though she keeps saying she doesn't want to talk about it.

"Not a day went by that I didn't think about you." I speak softly.

What was I thinking? It's taken me so long to feel something that's even slightly adjacent to okay without her. I fucking slept with Violette last night, and yet at the sound of Shay's voice I don't bend—I just break down.

"I . . . I miss you," I whisper. I cross the street quickly and roll up my sleeve to blot the tears forming in the corner of my eyes.

"I'm sorry we broke up." She stops. "I'm not sorry I left, because it's what I needed to do for my career, but I am sorry that I hurt you."

"I'm sorry too." I fall down on a park bench and stare skyward.

"Why didn't you call me?" she asks.

"I couldn't muster up the courage to," I reply.

"Tell me something new," Shay snaps. "You couldn't muster up the courage to come with me either." I can feel the resentment building again.

"This is the most ridiculous conversation we've ever had, huh." I laugh.

"Maybe we should finish it at another time?"

"Yes." I'm relieved that she's letting me off the hook.

Nelson's texts are coming in at rapid speed. He's gone from conversational to concerned in the span of five messages.

"Fucking Parker." Shay finally laughs.

"Fuck—ing Parker." I throw my fist up in the air.

"Taryn, I don't know what'll happen when I get back," she says.

My heart starts to thump in panic. "What do you mean?"

"I don't mean anything. I'm just saying, I don't know what'll happen," Shay answers. "Listen, I need to go."

"All right," I say, and hang up. Any enthusiasm I had about Shay has now turned to dread. Will we not get back together? Did I fuck up that badly by not going with her and not calling her? And what is she going to say when I tell her I slept with Violette . . .

Questions continue to plague me as I walk my way back to Nelson.

• • •

He meets me on the corner of Sixth Avenue and West Third Street. We take a stroll around the West Village, looking at the empty parks, and I catch him up on my conversation with Shay. We breeze past the West Fourth Street Courts, turn on West Fourth, and then make a right on MacDougal Street. When we reach Washington Square Park, there's a chess game going on between two men, both huddling in their coats. One of them, sporting a green fedora, is blowing heat from his mouth into his hands.

"She still fancy you?"

"Your guess is as good as mine."

"You tell her about your shag?"

"I didn't yet tell her, no." I shake my head, thinking about Parker's video. "Shay and I were robbed of our opportunity to tell our story." I take a deep inhale. Like a comeback that occurs to you well after the fight has ended, I make a confession of my own to Nelson: "I'm pissed off that our story is unraveling this way. But I will never forgive myself if I don't try to get her back now."

"You are making the assumption, Taryn, that her story and yours are still aligned."

"Why are you saying that our stories aren't aligned?"

We stand together in silence as I wait for his answer.

Nelson breaks our silence. "Will you tell her?"

"Of course I will. And it'll be over by then."

"You going to end things with Violette today?"

"Yes. Immediately. Today."

"I thought you said she was going back to Paris today?"

"I'll get on a plane and catch up with her and end it then. I'll do whatever I have to do to prove to Shay that it was a moment, nothing more."

Nelson laughs. "So you're going to get on a plane to end things?"

"I will if I have to, yes."

"The irony is uncanny. Shay invited you to travel and you didn't even so much as step on a plane for her, but you shagged a woman and you're willing to fly to break up with her?"

"I didn't think of it like that . . . but I feel like it sends Shay the right message, shows her how serious I am about her."

He nods his head. "This won't be the first terrible decision you've made when it comes to my sister, but I truly hope it will be the last."

We keep walking, and when the man in the green fedora yells "Checkmate," we can hear it from across the park.

Chapter 11
Après Moi, Le Déluge

Three Days Later

"You're missing Christmas?" Gwen asks again for the third time.

"No, I'll be back by Christmas Eve," I say into the phone, frantically throwing the items I left *to pack in the morning* into my bag. When I pass through airport security, I will inevitably remember the one thing I forgot because Gwen keeps making me repeat myself.

"Mom has been planning Christmas since Halloween. She bought a whole new holiday dish set this year, and she's been trying out recipes for over a month. You need to be here," she persists.

"Please, I know how disappointed she'll be if it I miss it, and unless there's an airline strike, I'll be back in time."

"Oh, this sounds interesting." I can hear her muffling a laugh.

"You promise you won't say anything? You won't tag me in anything? You won't put anything cryptic on your feed?"

"I promise," she says softly. "Where are you going?"

"I'm going to Paris."

"For Violette? Oh god, this is not a good idea! Does Violette know you're coming or is it a surprise situation?" She continues on without letting me get a word in: "I think you're right about not telling Mom. She wouldn't understand. You know how much she wishes you and Shay would work things out."

"No, no, no," I shove my passport into my backpack, "It's not what you think. I need to go to Paris to end things with Violette."

"Are kidding me?" Her voice raises a few decibels.

"Taryn, you had what, a few dates with her? Trust me, I know casual dating. You do not have to get on a plane this close to a holiday, or do any of this. In fact, you could probably get away with just calling her."

"I know," I sigh. "But I have miles racked up, and they're going to expire anyway."

"Uh-huh." Her voice exudes sarcasm.

"Look, I feel like this is the right thing to do."

"Okay, if you think it's right, then go. I, on the other hand, have actually changed my mind and think maybe even a text message is sufficient, considering it's the holidays and all."

"You are the worst." I zip up my carry-on and look at my watch. "I have to call a car. Please don't say anything."

"I won't." She hangs up on me.

The entire flight across the Atlantic Ocean, my mind is plagued with thoughts of Violette and Shay. Without Shay, for months, I had continued to feel hollow inside. My guitar started to gather dust because every chord reminded me of her. My music was too deeply attached to the memories of Shay's lips backstage, her excited smiles onstage, and the passion that danced in her eyes when we played.

And Violette. The intoxicating Violette filled in as the perfect savior for my aching heart. Her wildness pulled me out of the sorrow I had designed for myself. The sorrow which had pushed me to try and move on. But even a woman as enticing as Violette doesn't hold a candle to the space Shay occupies in my heart. Violette taught me to be brave enough to take a chance. Something I learned merely by sleeping with her.

When Air France Flight 107 touches down at Charles de Gaulle, I am awakened by the flight attendant announcing that the local time in Paris, France, is 8:06 p.m. My nap has refreshed my hopes that I am doing the right thing by ending things with Violette in person. My legs are weak and wobbly as I get up from my reclined seat. I struggle a bit navigating the airport signs, but eventually end up outside and walk straight to the middle divider to order a taxi.

Sitting in the back seat of the taxi, I call Violette and ask for her address. She sounds excited about my abrupt arrival in her country. I hang up and sigh. This can definitely be construed as spontaneous and romantic. Only I could fuck this up so badly. The trees are draped in twinkling lights, and colorful decorations are strung along the streets. They distract me from my concern that perhaps it was a terrible idea to come here.

Violette's hair is slicked back and coiled around the top of her head in an intricate knot when she opens the door. She seems warm and cheerful when she answers the door, gesturing for me to come into her apartment. The hallway is decorated with rustic antiques. Halfway down her very long and narrow hallway, she pulls me in for a hug and gives me kisses, one on each cheek. I slowly pull back and continue walking to the end of the hall, at the end of which I am greeted by a stuffed German shepherd. We walk into the grand parlor, and the first thing I notice on the ten-foot wall across from me is a piece of artwork. You would be hard-pressed to find this caliber of art in the US—a framed nineteenth-century sex scene—but in Paris, it seems like a typical occurrence.

Violette welcomes me into the kitchen and as she does, her cell phone rings. She answers and begins speaking very rapidly in French. When she hangs up, the only detail she offers me about the call is a smile. She turns up the volume on the stereo on the counter a little higher and begins humming the tune.

"Are you here for the holidays?" She looks down at my lack of a suitcase quizzically. "No luggage?"

"No. I'm not here for the holidays." I shake my head. "I have a flight back in eight hours."

She raises an eyebrow, pulls two wine glasses from the cabinet, and places them on the large central island.

"Can I put my coat down somewhere?" I begin to remove it, one sleeve at a time.

"Of course, *chérie*." Her pitch goes up at the end of her sentence in a bit of excitement.

I take my coat off and she takes it from me to hang it up in the hallway near the front door.

"You had it dry cleaned." She notes the lack of specs from the fire extinguisher.

I smile at her, warmed by the notion that we have a shared memory. "I did."

I peek out into the living room where a brilliant white seven-foot tree is decorated in only blue sequins, beads, balls, and bows. Presents are littered underneath it, and for a moment, I wonder if one is for me.

Violette pulls out a bottle from the bar, places it on the ledge above, and continues her search for one bottle of wine in particular. My eyes dart around the kitchen and settle on the various copper pots and pans hanging above the island. She unlatches and pulls back the French doors (are they simply doors here?), revealing a balcony off the kitchen that I hadn't noticed until now. She steps out onto it and motions for me to follow. She walks to the far right side of the circular balcony and points out at the Eiffel Tower; its green and red lights are shimmering like a vertical version of the Northern Lights. I take a deep breath. It's not the first time my eyes drink up the glittering sight of the Eiffel Tower, yet seeing it here, with her, makes it new just the same.

She breaks our steady silence after lighting a cigarette. "I like to immediately invite my visitors out here."

Feeling slightly dejected at having been reduced to a visitor, I stand still, wishing I had just called instead. I'm several feet away from Violette, arms crossed and jaw clenched a little from the cold. A part of me desires to go back to the nights we got to know each other and undo them all. I hold my gaze up to the brilliant sky to hide the tears that have formed. I discreetly wipe my eyes. She flicks away what's left of her cigarette and motions for me to follow her back inside. She picks up the two glasses that she took out earlier, looks out into the distance for a moment, and then arrests her thoughts and pours wine into both glasses.

"I shouldn't have come here." I confess through slightly wet eyes.

She turns her head and looks at me in a way that is totally askew. "Why do I have a feeling that you are not here for fun?" She hands me a glass.

I swish the liquid around before taking a swig. "Shay is coming home."

She puts her glass down and opens her engraved platinum cigarette carrier again. "*Je suis désolée.*" She nods at the case, offering me a cigarette this time, but I decline by waving her off. "You are mad right now because you don't want to admit that you shouldn't have slept with me when you loved someone else."

"I'm not mad. It's just that . . ." I shake my head.

She stands taller, waiting.

"You were the first woman I was with since Shay left. Do you know how hard that was for me? To finally take the chance to be with someone else."

"Hard," she scoffs. "I am sorry, *mon amour*, but being with me didn't seem like much of a challenge for you." She runs her hand down the side of my face.

I turn my lips into the palm of her hand, then reluctantly pull back.

With her other hand, she holds her cigarette straight up so the ashes don't fall and breaks off from me to search for an ashtray. "Taryn," she says, pronouncing my name *Tah-rin* as she becomes more flustered. "You don't even know what you are chasing."

I find a small glass ashtray to the right of me on the counter. I walk over and hand it to her. "I'm not chasing anything."

She drops her ash into the glass vessel and nods in gratitude as she takes it from me. She takes a deep drag, exhales, and looks up to watch the smoke. "You are so insulting, it's almost painful, *chérie*." She puts the cigarette out dramatically. "You came all the way here to tell me you don't want me? As what, a twisted Christmas present?"

"This might have been terrible judgment on my part," I whisper.

"Things were never meant to be so serious between you and I," she admits. "I did tell you that I wanted

127

something deeper, and I meant it at the time. But *chérie*, I didn't realize you loved her so dearly . . ." She shakes her head in pity for me and picks up her glass of wine from the counter for a sip.

"Neither did I." There's something about my pointed anger—it's so direct—yet it's not for Violette.

I recoil when the tears fall down her face. Memories flash of dragging my fingertips across her flesh from one spot to another. Pulling her hair. Pressing my lips against hers, connecting the dots between each spot I knew would make her beg for more. I intuitively knew when to apply pressure or when to ease up, when to kiss her breasts gently or to pull her on top of me.

Yet, as I stand in her kitchen near the wide-open doors of the balcony—from which a large gust of wind has just blown in—I connect another set of dots, dots that I had never connected before. How gutted I was when Shay left is a dot. Pursuing Violette was a dot. Then the final dot, the one that reveals it all, is connected, burned, shot right into my gut. Now it boils, with acidic undertones, right up to my heart. My recent obsession with getting my band back together is nothing else if not a loosely veiled metaphor for wanting Shay back. It's the final dot.

"Thank you for the wine and the memories, but I think I should probably leave."

"Leave? But you just got here, to Paris." She looks attentively into her glass as if the solution to world peace is inscribed on the bottom.

"I know but—" I grab her hand. "I just needed to see you in person because I care deeply for you. A little more than I had planned to."

My eyes dart from her shiny hair to her lips and down her cleavage. Wow, she is beautiful. A person can be beautiful and nothing more. I once held her beauty. Now I hold her as just a beautiful person—but not *my* beautiful person.

She puts her wine glass down and takes my other hand in hers. Goosebumps immediately form on my arms when she does. I close my eyes tight, and when I open them, tears threaten to spill over my lashes. Even though I've hardened myself to stop their flow, they fall fast. It would be a travesty for me to admit that these tears are for her. She pulls me in close and I hold her firm body like a secret, but quickly pull back. Despite the little time we spent together, I know she belongs to Paris, and she knows I belong to Shay. There is something permanent and real about my tears, but there's nothing everlasting about Violette and I.

I take a mental picture of the parts I hope I'll never forget but know, eventually, that I will. The problem with sleeping with a woman like Violette is that the intensity eventually burns out, but you never do forget how hot it was.

The music pipes up a little louder, or at least I notice it more. And as far as irony goes, "La Vie en Rose" playing on the surround sound as you and your faux French girlfriend break up is about as classic as it gets.

My emotions are shot. I end up sleeping on the flight back to NYC. When I wake up in the morning, I see that the flight attendant has left a tiny chocolate in a blue box on my tray table with a tag that reads, *With love, from Paris.*

Chapter 12
Before This Time Another Year

Christmas at Mom's went off as one would expect: an orgy of presents, a smattering of baked goods, and as is our tradition every year on Christmas Day, Mom carefully removed one of my father's records from its sleeve and placed it on the record player. Every December 25th, we invite him to join us in the only way that's available to us—his music. The greatest love of my mom's life exists only on vinyl.

Perhaps the best gifts we exchanged were when Gwen told Mom that I narrowly missed Christmas because I went to Paris to end things with Violette, so in return, I told Mom that Gwen has a boyfriend who she seems to be getting serious with. It felt right that Mom was skeptical about my tattling: Gwen's always been a bit—ambitious—when it comes to finding love. She runs a dating catch-and-release program where she catches men, reels them in, pulls them out of the water completely, and then lets them loose. I don't have enough free space in my brain to remember all the names of the men she's dated. If a man is a total flake, maybe has a few kids but never pays child support, and is always working on some entrepreneurial deal that borders on illegality, Gwen gravitates toward him like a moth to a flame.

Since I know these men won't be around long, I generally give them ridiculous nicknames. "Karma" is a guy who banged on the passenger-side door of her car, screaming that "karma" was going to get her for breaking his heart. Then there's "Yellow Speedo," a guy who did Bikram yoga wearing only tight yellow briefs. I want so badly to give Bradley a moniker, and yet I already know I shouldn't, that there's something different about him. During Christmas dinner, Mom got increasingly suspicious about Gwen's claims of how serious her relationship with Bradley is, being that he wasn't there with us for the holidays. To prove it, Gwen insisted that I join her the next day at one of Bradley's races.

And so, here we are.

• • •

"I've never been to a snow bike race, but I've always wanted to go to one. This feels like a scene I can get into," I tell Gwen as we walk through the stands, looking for a good spot to sit.

This is like Gwen's fifth race and she thinks she's basically an expert on the subject matter. I told her, "Going to his race this soon is a little thirsty," but she disregarded my advice.

I watch intently as Bradley shifts his body forward on his snow bike. I only know the name of it because every time I call it a motocross bike, Gwen vehemently corrects me, "Motocross is when he's racing on dirt; a snow bike is when he's racing on snow."

Nineteen riders, including Bradley, face the countdown board as the numbers descend from sixty. None of the racers turn their head left or right. They might move a foot or lift a hand, but their helmets remain steadfastly forward. The clock strikes zero and Bradley peels out on the snow and launches in front of the pack. They climb hills in a rhythmic formation so routine that if you listen closely you can hear the melody of it all: rev, speed, catch air, jump, land, and then do it all again. Bradley hits another set of jumps and gains speed. Gwen and I watch intently as he soars through the air and snow flies everywhere.

"Who's number forty-nine? He's on Bradley's ass!" Gwen yells out to the crowd. But it doesn't matter that number forty-nine is stalking him—nothing shatters Bradley's concentration. I can't see his reactions under his helmet's face guard, but I bet his expression is totally serious. In the crowd, the same amateur riders who were just taking selfies are now standing still and watching the pros intently.

When Bradley inches ahead of the other eighteen riders, he turns his head to look behind him.

"Why!" Gwen screams. "Don't look back," she urges him from the stands. She complains, "If he keeps looking back, he's going to lose," as if she's got money riding on this race.

On the inside of the final turn, Bradley passes everyone else. He flies through the air and small tornadoes of snow dust form around him and his bike.

A few yards beyond the finish line, Bradley hovers over his bike and we run toward him. He takes off his helmet and goggles and wipes the sweat from his face. Gwen goes to hug him and then stops in her tracks—his uniform is covered with snow. He hangs his helmet from his handlebars and walks his bike in the direction of a line of pickup trucks. When we pass the water table, he grabs a bottle. Gwen smiles at him, and he tells her he has a change of clothes in his truck. Gwen and I stop, not knowing which row of trucks we're heading toward, and Bradley points us in the right direction, chugging down his bottle of water in one shot.

"I'm happy you were able to come, Taryn," he says as he tosses the empty bottle into a recycling bin.

I smirk. "Anything for my big sis."

I make my way through the crowd, headed for the parking lot faster than Gwen and Bradley because I'm not maneuvering a bike; also, I want to give them some time to talk privately, since Bradley's headed to Virginia after this, and Gwen is coming back to Queens with me. A tiny woman, maybe a third of Bradley's size, screams so loud that the shrill echoes through the air for several moments, causing me, Gwen, and Bradley to freeze and our heads to turn, one by one, like dominoes in her direction.

"I know you!" The screamer points aggressively at me, her voice ragged. I instinctively want to look behind me, but this has recently become a routine event. Parker's album with not one but two consecutive hits has made Pause For Effect's star shine even brighter. Being spotted in public should feel like a privilege, but for me it's becoming a burden.

"You were in that band, the one Parker used to be in."

It's going to be a long day, I think. I smile at her, long enough for it to feel awkward. Gwen grabs me by the shoulder and spins me around fast enough to break my gaze. I blink at my sister. "I love how my band has been reduced to 'the band Parker used to be in.'"

Gwen nods at me, opens her mouth to say something, but the guy in the number forty-nine jersey rushes up to Bradley, tousles his hair, and yells, "You wanna let someone else win for a change?" He puts his arms up in a letter *V* as he runs past.

Now, Bradley is so far ahead that he stops to wait for us. We pick up the pace and he parks his bike alongside his crimson pickup truck. The bike's custom matte black paint job contrasts well with the red fireballs painted on the seat. Metallic flecks make the fireballs glitter slightly when the sun hits them at a certain angle. Bradley peels off his outer layer and gently places his helmet and goggles down. He jumps up into the bed of the truck and pulls out a metal ramp. Gwen hands him a necklace of black satin string with a long cylinder at the end of it, and he kisses her hand.

Another rider, number seven on his jersey, walks by. "See you at the podium, Collins," he commands. Bradley squints from the sun and laughs. "I don't need another trophy."

• • •

Bradley's not within earshot so I ask Gwen, "What was that necklace you just gave him?"

She turns to me. "His mother's ashes. He wears them."

"Oh." I pucker my lips, not sure of what to say. "He takes her off when he rides?"

"Every race." She walks to the front of the pickup and moves out the side-view mirror. Naturally, she begins to reapply her makeup.

"Taryn," Bradley calls, pulling down the back gate of the bed, "you want to help me load my bike onto the truck?" He instructs me to "Grab that end," motioning with his chin to the far end of the ramp. I grab one end, and he leans the other against the back gate. Then we push his bike up the ramp onto the bed, the truck groaning a little under the burden of the weight. He loads the bike in diagonal across the bed of his truck, leaning the bike a little to the left as he begins to tie down the right side. He motions for me to lean the bike toward him and pulls the tie until it's firm and tight.

"Hey, so, do you get that a lot? People calling it Parker's old band?"

"Do you know how much it took out of me to politely walk away from her?" I ask.

"Normally, no matter what's happening, bad day, bad relationship, whatever, I think about riding and it all drifts away. I just think about jumping on the bike and everything is gravy. The speed feels so good rushing through me. I commit to the first turn. Then I commit to the next jump." He leans the bike in the opposite direction and pulls the tie away from him.

I can only nod my head. I can't form words. It's like he knows that playing in a band is my religion—my way to stay in the moment—my race. I close my eyes tight and hold back tears. The sun dips down behind the trees, and light peers through the cracks as if playing peekaboo with a toddler.

He finishes securing all the tie-downs and jumps out of the truck. He puts his hand up, I grab it, and he helps me down to the ground. Then he pulls a bag out of the cab of his truck and shoves his helmet and gear into it.

"Hey, sorry we missed you for Christmas." I look back to see if Gwen is going to give me side-eye for bringing up the holidays.

"I'm sorry I missed it too. I have races all this week, my schedule is nuts. I'm so happy you agreed to come out with Gwen. I was worried I wasn't going to see her at all."

I push my agenda a little more. "So do you usually spend the holidays with your family, or—?"

He flings his bag onto the bed of the trunk and stands up tall. "I'm not sure if Gwen told you, but I don't have a very big family. It's not all coincidence that I busy myself with races this time of year."

I can see that Gwen's cocked her head to the side a little, and she'll kill me if I press on, so I stop the inquisition. "Thank you so much for inviting me. This was fun. I definitely want to come to another one." I smile.

"Thanks for coming out, Taryn." He embraces me in a sideways hug, which is perfect. We aren't yet close enough for a full-frontal hug but we need an embrace more meaningful than a handshake. The hug is close enough for me to take in his cologne. It's fruity with woody overtones.

"Maybe when I get Pause For Effect back together we can do like, a tour, with bands and motocross stars and—"

He and I laugh. "Like the Warped Tour," we say at the same time.

"Hey, I really like your sister." I feel the expectant pressure of Bradley's eyes trained on me. I am struck by his confession—it rings so real, a prospect more exciting to me on behalf of Gwen than I ever could have imagined.

• • •

Gwen's car reeks of the scent of Bradley's cologne. Her back seat, with clothes and heels strewn about, reminds me of a teenager's bedroom floor. I'm not fully convinced that the car, which was once a college graduation gift, isn't now doubling as a home. Gwen weaves in and out of lanes.

"I really like him for you!" I tell her.

"The Taryn stamp of approval isn't easy to come by." She lowers the volume of the music from a control on her steering wheel.

"Not with the men you've dated, that's for sure."

"Yeah, Bradley is pretty awesome. But speaking of men that aren't awesome, what the fuck was up with that Parker video?"

"I don't want to talk about Parker." I stare out the window.

Gwen mistakes my silence as a cue to continue. "So he's like, never coming back to the band, is he?"

"Gwen," I warn, shaking my head, "not now."

"So, how was Paris?"

"Exactly what I needed it to be: quick and dirty."

"Ohhhhh, sounds so scandalous! My little sister, traversing the globe to clean up the sexcapades in Shay's wake right before she returns."

"It was hardly scandalous, more like anticlimactic."

"I was right, wasn't I, about Violette?"

"What, that she's your standard issue temptress: French and seductive?"

"No, that you shouldn't have flown to Paris!" Her hand glides around the wheel.

"Ugh, yes." The leather creaks as I shift in my seat. "You were right."

"I know a thing or two about dating."

I look down at my phone. "Fuck, fuck, fuck, fuck, fuck me!" I yell.

"What?" She swerves over the double yellow lines.

"Fucking Sofia Alexi."

"Oh," she exhales. "Don't fucking do that me while I'm driving." She smacks my arm. "I thought it was something important."

"This *is* important. This horrible woman is threatening to publish a photo of me and Violette from Chloe's 78."

"Let me see." She pulls the car over and takes my phone from my hand.

"How did she get this? Security is so tight at that place." She hands me back my phone. "Anyway, let her do it. You look hot."

"Seriously? That's not the point."

She peels out and gets back on the road. "Why? Who cares? You're all adults, you had a fling, and now you're on to some other thing. No big deal."

"Sofia Alexi is going to be the death of me."

"She will not be the death of you unless you let her."

"I just flew to Paris to end things with Violette, and now Shay is going to see this."

"Doesn't Shay already know about Violette?"

"I didn't exactly tell her yet."

"Wow, you just follow up terrible decisions with absolutely awful decisions, Taryn."

"As Nelson says, I'm somewhat of a prodigy."

"You should use this lady you hate to your advantage."

"How do you mean?"

"All these years in the music business and you know nothing."

"What do you mean, I know nothing?"

"Sofia Alexi clearly wants your attention, so give it to her and get in front of this. Call her up, tell her you have something for her, something so much better than a dumb photo of you and your one-time tryst."

I stop clicking on my phone and look up at Gwen. "That's actually not the dumbest idea you've ever had."

"Thank you, thank you very much." She nods and smiles.

"I'm going to call Sofia Alexi and tell her I want to give her an exclusive interview."

"There you go, take control of your story." She pumps her arm in the air.

I smile at Gwen, knowing that one thing is true: if I can get Sofia Alexi to give me airtime, I will tell the world about Violette, so no one else can.

Chapter 13

By the Light of the Silvery Moon

2012

It's New Year's Eve, and the streets outside SLZ Media are swollen with onlookers and tourists wearing 2012-themed hats and glasses, waiting to watch the countdown outside the fishbowl-like studio. The outdoor overhead lighting brilliantly illuminates the crowd as if it were midday. Fans stand among them, holding up homemade signs that read, *Pause For Effect 4Ever* and *We <3 you Taryn*. The crowd is noticeably still, perhaps because they're packed closely together within the barricades, wearing thick jackets, gloves, and several scarves. The many layers of clothing may restrict their mobility, but they don't dampen their screams. Their enthusiasm reminds me of what the crowd sounded like as the lights went down at one of our shows. The clamoring fans bring me back to a place I long to be.

"The *Live and Uncut* interview will take place in front of a live audience," Sofia explains. She's said this script hundreds of times before; it's obvious by the way she rushes through the details. I'd watched dozens of hours of ball drops in my life, and I know the type of nonsense space-filler interviews that generally play out to fill up time before the countdown. I also know my interview will not be one of them.

One of the show's producers walks Gwen and me around the place. She barely takes her eyes off her cell, occasionally referencing a clipboard or replying to someone in her headset, but manages to point out where the dressing rooms, bathrooms, and craft services are located.

"Is there a makeup mirror in the dressing room?" Gwen asks the producer, who just points to the room again as she talks into her headset, responding to someone else's question at the same time.

"I need to do your war paint!" Gwen tells me, looking down at her watch and motioning to the dressing room.

"Yeah."

We go in and I sit down in a director-type chair.

"Are you ready?" Gwen asks.

"Yes, let's do it."

She pats my face with concealer and then retrieves a brush from what I have dubbed Pandora's Box. She blows into the center of the brush to remove any stray hairs and dips it into powder. She instructs me to close my eyes and lightly powders my nose and cheeks.

"How much time do we have?" I yell. Having my eyes closed makes me feel the need to yell.

"About twenty minutes," Gwen shouts back before blowing into what must be another brush. "Open your eyes," she demands, and turns my head from left to right, admiring her work. "I honestly hope you're successful at whatever it is you are trying to accomplish here today." She applies mascara to my left eyelashes.

"I told you, Gwen. Just trust me. It's going to be epic."

She dips the stick back into its black vessel and applies it to my right eyelashes. "Well, I certainly hope the tea you're going to spill is worth all the mystery."

"Just trust me."

"Close your mouth."

"No, you close your mouth!" I yell.

Gwen laughs. "Close your mouth so I can put lipstick on you."

I grin as I acquiesce.

"Okay, I'm done with you," she declares as she packs up her makeup. I look into the mirror and check the end result. Gwen made sure to keep it simple, knowing that I don't like too much makeup . She's given me a soft nude lip and natural-looking eyes. I look up to her, perhaps seeking her approval, and she winks and smirks in response.

Gwen looks down at her phone and smiles. "It's Bradley, he wishes you luck!"

I smile back. "Tell him I wish him a Happy New Year."

"I hope he doesn't think he's going to get away with avoiding the holidays every year," she quips. "I let him get away with it this year because I didn't want to be 'that woman,' but I'm putting my foot down next year."

"So you think he'll be around next year?" It comes out way harsher than intended.

"You're such a jerk."

I laugh. "I promise you, that is not how I meant it." The heat of the room makes tiny beads of sweat gather on my forehead and upper lip, and I wipe them away.

"No, do not wipe like that!" Gwen yells. She hands me an oil-absorbent sheet. "Pat. You gently pat your face."

The show's producer pops her head into our dressing room. "Ten minutes till we're live!" She motions for me to come with her to escort me to my space on the stage.

I stand up straight and pull at the revealing sweater I'm wearing. Gwen runs over to smooth it out.

"Do you really think I need to let the girls out like this?" I pull the V-neck opening higher up my cleavage. As we walk toward to the studio, Gwen taps my hand every time I try to rearrange the neck again.

The producer gives me a brief rundown as I settle into the couch on the stage. "That's camera one"—the assistant points—"that's two and three"—she flings her arm out. "One will be the camera we use most. The red light on top indicates that it's on." She hoists a microphone wire up my shirt. "Who am I kidding; you've probably done hundreds of interviews, haven't you?" she asks. I laugh and smile. "I was trying to be polite."

The bright lights of the set for *Live and Uncut* are eclipsed by the screaming applause of three hundred fans who really seem to miss Pause For Effect. And maybe they even miss me. I know these shows sometimes bring in fake audiences, but I can tell these are the real deal. These are *ours*, and they all know me. Being in front of crowds fifty times this size is old hat, and yet this borders on scary. My breath does this weird thing in my lungs where it causes a bit of back pain when I try to catch it.

Sofia Alexi enters the set, extends her hand for me to shake, and then settles in the chair across from me, grinning a grin that either means "Sorry about all this" or "I am going to destroy you." One can never tell with her.

Someone from behind the camera speaks up: "Ten seconds to live." They count down the rest of the seconds on their fingers, and when the last finger drops, Sofia announces, "Welcome back to the show! We know you've been waiting too long for this moment, so let's welcome our guest for tonight, Taryn from Pause For Effect!"

I smile and wave to the audience. After the whooping finally calms down, Sofia turns to me. "So, Taryn," she starts, "thanks for coming to *Live and Uncut*."

"I'm glad to be here, Sofia," I lie.

"How do you feel about Pause For Effect's breakup and Parker's solo success?

"Well, Pause For Effect is simply on hiatus." I shift in my seat. "And I truly want nothing more than Parker's success." I can't help but sneak a look at Gwen's face, and it's priceless. I wish I could take a shot of her expression right now, a mixture of disbelief and amusement.

Sofia laughs a hearty laugh. I grin as she frantically tries to come back to center and get back into interview mode.

"Well, success is what he's found!" Her eyes are shooting daggers at me. "And his new video. It seems a bit—" She pauses to pretend to find the right words. "It's a little bit personal his new video." Her shoulders dance a little, like they're unable to contain the excitement flowing within her.

"Oh," I laugh politely, "yeah, Parker really loves to stir the pot. Bit of a drama queen, that one."

Sofia crosses one leg over the other. "And how do you feel about the fans' reaction to the video? I'm sure the lovely fans in our audience enjoyed it as well." She's pandering to the crowd to solicit applause from them. "Inquiring minds want to know. Is the video at all reminiscent of real life?"

Sweat moistens my forehead and I want so badly to wipe it, but I look out at Gwen and know she will rush this stage if I do, so I ignore the sweat and my palpitating heart.

"Well, let's survey the crowd." I look out at the audience. "Did anyone here love Parker's video?" The screams and hollers from the audience drown out my voice.

I nod and smile, proud that I deflected her question.

Like a good journalist, she moves on, but I know she'll figure out how to circle back to it. "So what has Taryn been doing while the band is broken up?" She smirks. "Or should I have said, *who* has Taryn been doing?"

"Well, we're on a break, we're not broken up." I feel the tension starting to build. "I've been writing a lot of new material." I look out to the crowd, and when the cheers die down, I continue: "And I did some traveling. I recently went to Paris."

"Oh, *oui, oui!* Did you find it inspirational for songwriting?"

"I most certainly found it inspiring, yes."

"The French, they can be anyone's muse," Sofia purrs.

"Paris is a city known for love." I play right into her hands and give her the bait. I wait anxiously to see if she takes it.

"And did you fall in love in Paris?"

Three, two, one, Houston, we have liftoff. I look out at Gwen. She nods her head at me.

"Look," I glance down at my feet and then stand up. Production people are running back to their posts to follow me with their cameras as I walk to the front of the stage.

"Sofia, you want a story, and I'm going to give you a story."

"Oh!" She claps nervously. "An exclusive!" she yells out to crowd.

"The truth is, Sofia—" I'm speaking really fast and my words are jumbled. I'm nervous that I'm fucking this whole plan up. Camera one finally figures out its rhythm and stays trained on me as I walk slowly across the stage. "Parker's video is one hundred percent true. Shay and I were a couple for our entire career. And I made a really awful mistake." I can tell Sofia wants to jump in and ask a follow-up question. She raises the microphone to her mouth but I don't give her the chance. "I fucked up." I laugh. "Oops, sorry, can you say 'fuck' on this show?"

Sofia laughs and I continue before she can hijack me. "I love Shay with every fiber of my being, and while Pause For Effect was taking a break, I should've been with her. I should've supported her passion for photography. I should've been a better girlfriend. I lost months of my life with her. And now I'll do anything—even go on shows like this—where, no offense, Sofia, I really would rather not ever appear—to profess my love to her."

"Wow, Taryn, that's really—wow." Sofia looks out at the crowd and speaks directly to them. "That was a lot to digest, right?" She conjures up their applause by starting to clap first. "And speaking of breaking up . . ." She looks back at me now. "I heard a rumor that you were in Paris this week breaking up with someone else." She's frantically flipping through her note cards. "Is there any truth to this rumor? That even though you profess to love Shay, you were actually with someone else?"

Gotcha! is what I think she wants to shout at me for screwing up her interview.

"Oh," I laugh, "that was hardly a relationship. I've had manicurists that I've had more intimate relationships with." My eyes are trained on camera one, and camera one is trained on me. "I saw the woman who I really love having a great time in her life, chasing her dreams, and I was jealous. The biggest mistake I made in this whole ordeal was trying to be a rock star's rock star, which I am not. I never meant to hurt . . ." I decide to forgo using Violette's name. ". . . I never meant to hurt anyone. Shay especially."

I look directly into camera one. "Shay, if you're watching this"—my voice catches in my throat a little—"I am so sorry."

"Now you kind of have the whole story." I shrug to the audience.

The crowd is roaring with applause. There's foot-stomping and hollering. Sofia can barely get them to calm down. The clapping eventually dies down, and the producer holds up a cue card that reads, *You need to start the countdown.*

Sofia regains her composure. "Taryn, we don't have a lot of time, but I need to ask the real question on everyone's mind. How do you feel about Parker's announcement that he was just in rehab for thirty days?"

"Rehab?" The word comes out so fast that I can't pretend that I knew this. I cannot formulate a plan on the spot to play this off. And as the seconds elapse, I worry that my gaping mouth and quizzical expression will reveal how completely out of Parker's inner circle I am—because, I am!

The producer is holding up cue card after cue card demanding that Sofia get to the New Year's countdown. She shifts her body away from me and looks directly into camera two.

"Looks like it's time for the countdown! Ten, nine, eight, seven, six, five, four, three, two, one—Happy New Year!"

Chapter 14
Just a Little Drink

Gwen rushes me out the back door of SLZ Media to the parking lot, where the valet fetches her car. Once out of the garage, she guns it, her tires screeching.

I don't say a word to her—I'm glued to my phone. And there it is.

It broke just ten minutes before I went live with Sofia. Comment after comment on his post about having just finished a thirty-day program. *Bringing in the new year with a sober outlook and alcohol-free sparkling cider,* reads the caption under his photo.

"People usually brag when they go into rehab," I say. "I can't believe he's bragging that he just got out of one."

The speedometer needle tears past seventy. "I can't believe it's been so long since you've spoken to him that he could go to rehab without telling you."

"Please watch the road," I yell at her.

Gwen attempts to merge into the next lane without a signal and I push down on a fictitious brake on the floor.

"I guess that has been the theme of the year for me."

"What?" She again crosses lanes without a signal.

"Me not speaking to members of my band or knowing the intimate details of their lives."

"Or them, yours."

"Touché."

She incessantly honks her horn at the driver in front of her who didn't immediately release the brake when the light changed color. Then she yells at a car that cuts in front of us: "Go, just, go."

"Gwen, it's still New Year's Eve night. You should be driving more carefully. A lot of drunk people are probably on the road."

She eases up on the accelerator.

"Why are you driving like a mad woman?"

Her tires come to screeching halt on Tenth Avenue, just outside a 1920s-themed speakeasy. It's an underground bar and not easy to get into, unless you know the right people or are the right people. I've always wanted to find a way to get in but never have. I wanted to come with Shay but never did, and then I didn't want to come with anyone else.

"Go inside, Shay's waiting for you." Gwen points to the building.

I look down at myself, suddenly conscious of my outfit, my hair, my makeup.

"Your tits look great," Gwen jokes about my cleavage-revealing top.

I give her a sullen stare.

"I'm serious, you look awesome." Gwen unlocks my door. "Now go!"

A bouncer in a 2012 top hat nods at me as I walk straight past him and head inside.

• • •

A woman wearing a feather boa reaches behind her and pushes down on a lever, and the damask wall to my right splits in two. A boisterous crowd is hidden inside the speakeasy. There's not a light bulb in the place over thirty-five watts. A drunken man in search of his seat nearly knocks me to the floor as he clumsily sits down at his table. It's acceptable, encouraged even, to be falling down drunk on New Year's Eve. I glance around the room. Everyone is sauced to some degree except for me, and maybe even Shay.

I smile at her from afar, drinking her in. She's dressed in all black. Her hair is in a high ponytail. I find myself inhaling and exhaling deeply before I reach her. She flashes me a smile, familiar as the smell before rain. We launch into each other for an embrace that might be the longest we've ever held in public. The hug is far more intimate than I was expecting, and her signature vanilla scent triggers instant comfort.

Shay is first to pull away. She clears her throat and gestures for me to follow her through the bar.

It's bizarre, the way you still feel seamlessly connected with someone you adore despite the passage of time. Love allows you to pick up emotionally wherever you last left off.

The chandeliers hanging above us don't prevent the big band sounds from flowing up the walls and across the ceiling. In every cozy corner, couples are canoodling on plush velvet love seats. I reach out to take Shay's hand, and she lets me hold it as we head toward a private U-shaped booth, a space where the spotlight won't be on us—in fact, barely any lights will be on us. Within moments a suspender-wearing gent is standing in front of our table, waiting for our order.

Shay, who has clearly already identified what we'll have, orders "a Plum Bullet" for herself "and a Schultz" for me.

"And they say chivalry is dead."

She settles into the booth, scooting a little bit closer to me, finally laughing quietly at my comment. "There's burlesque here on Sundays and Tuesdays."

"It's a Monday, so all the women have their clothes on." I snicker.

It's a private space and I appreciate that all eyes are not on us, but my eyes are definitely on Shay. I take my jacket off to get more comfortable, shove it into a corner of the booth, and there's still plenty of room to spare.

I give in to the lure of her gaze. Her eyelids are perfectly adorned with a smoky composition that makes her golden eyes twinkle. It is ridiculous that she spends so much time behind a camera when she's as beautiful as any model who's stood in front of one.

"So how does it feel to be back?"

"It feels about eighty percent familiar and twenty percent jarring to know I'll be sleeping in the same place night after night for the foreseeable future." She cracks a small smile.

"And where will you be sleeping night after night?"

"I'm staying with Nelson for now until I find a place."

"You can always stay with me at my Mom's," I offer.

She looks down at the table, perhaps to break the weight of my unabashed stare (I can't help it, she's too gorgeous), and then looks back up at me.

The waiter places our drinks in front of us with exact precision. We take our first sip in tandem, and I note that she does not take me up on my offer of free lodging.

Always mindful of her surroundings, Shay looks around before she gets into it: "I saw your interview."

With little to no concern for our privacy, I speak much louder than I intend to: "Did Gwen give you a heads-up to watch it?"

Shay shifts in her seat. "She might have coordinated all of this, yes."

"But she didn't know what I was going to say."

"I guess she's got killer sister instincts."

I bring my voice down a few decibels. "I meant every word I said."

"Did you orchestrate the entire interview, or was any of it left to chance?" She tilts her head to the side. "And expose our relationship, and talk about some other woman . . . and . . . and . . ."

"I always knew I was going to tell the world that I love you, yes."

"And did you mean it, about not knowing Parker went to rehab?"

"I haven't spoken to him since the video dropped. Did you know?" I shoot back.

"Parker is the least of my priorities right now." She laughs. "And no, I didn't know."

"What is your priority?" I ask.

"I am." She looks down at her drink and takes a sip.

"I thought we'd discuss it together, in person, as a unified front with him, but now that you're here, in front of me, in person, nothing seems less important than addressing Parker."

"Well, I admit," she smirks, "it was nice seeing you squirm a little and professing your love to me."

I smile wide. "Did I finally do something right?"

"I am excited," She pauses. "I'm excited to tell you about my exhibit."

"Will I be invited to the opening?"

"Of course! You'll be my date." She snickers.

"Too soon for the dating jokes." I sigh. What a grueling place we're in, not to know whether we can or should consider ourselves fodder for jokes about our relationship.

She nods. "I'm sorry." A stillness falls over the booth, one so heavy that I want to make quietly for the door, but do not.

I move slowly but methodically back to the topic of us. "You have no idea how much I missed you," I confess.

"So much that you that you, how do I say it in French, *slept with someone else?*" Her comment reflects a manufactured feeling of indifference.

"Oh please, we are not going there," I chide.

"Taryn—" She slides her pinky finger into her ring and bends it. "I know our relationship wasn't perfect, but it would be nice for us to finally talk about how it all fell apart."

"I know. But I don't want to know who you were fucking, when you were in Lithuania or wherever the fuck," I laugh.

"It wasn't Lithuania, but we should talk about Pause For Effect playing in Lithuania, because we're huge there." She extends her arms to show the scope of our popularity.

"We would have to get back together for that to happen."

I grab her hand and fold her fingers over mine. Her hand is warm, and its touch seems to tingle slightly.

" 'We' as in 'us,' or the royal 'we,' the band?"

Shay laughs. "Oh, the band. And maybe we can play Paris too." She gives me a bit of side-eye through her long lashes.

"I went to end things with her," I quickly respond.

"So it was serious enough for you to go all the way across the ocean?"

I take a soft breath before answering. "I was wrong about that part. It made it seem much more serious than it was. Gwen was right."

"Gwen told you to go?"

"Gwen told me not to go."

"And that's why I love Gwen." She nods.

"Shay, I need you to be honest with me." My heartbeat speeds up a few ticks.

"I'm honest." She pulls my left hand and holds it out.

She places her ring onto my ring finger. When she touches my hand, I feel the hair on the back of my neck raise up.

"Is it really over with you and the woman you were seeing?" I say all of this indifferently, as if it's cool either way—but really, it's not.

She steals a surreptitious glance at me, and then another. I want so badly to kiss her.

"Well, since you've just come back from Paris, I'll use a metaphor you'll recognize right away." She winks. "You've been to the Eiffel Tower, yes?" She glances down and admires the ring on my hand.

"Well, I've been three times, and twice was with you on tour, so you know the answer is yes."

"And remember how beautiful the Eiffel Tower is from the Seine?"

"Gorgeous. Absolutely stunning." I hold my fingers in front of my face to pantomime a camera.

"And how about from directly underneath the Eiffel Tower? Is the view as breathtaking?"

"Directly underneath?"

"Right, directly underneath. Where we bought our tickets."

"From that angle, you can see the true integrity of the structure, some of the cracks—"

She interrupts me. "The woman I was seeing is like the Eiffel Tower. I should have viewed her only from the Seine and not any closer."

"Or not at all?" I ask.

"Or not at all," she reassures me as she takes another swallow of her drink. She looks at her watch. "I have to get going soon. You would not believe the amount of prep work I have left to do for my exhibit."

"We lead the kind of lives where, if nothing happens in one moment, you wait for another and everything completely changes. Can we have one last drink?" I shift in my seat. She nods.

I raise my hand to get the waiter's attention. He walks over and when he gets to our table, he furiously cleans a non-existent spill.

"Do you think it's possible that we can have another Plum Bullet and a Schultz?"

He nods his head but stares a hole through my chest.

"Is it also possible that you can stop ogling my breasts?"

"Sorry," Shay says half-jokingly to the waiter. Looking slightly sheepish, he turns away and heads back toward the bar.

"This is probably as good a time as any to mention that I got an offer to put out a book of portraits."

"What!" I exclaim. Conscious of my yelling, I bring the volume down. "Congrats!"

Her warm eyes look deep into mine and she offers me her soft smile. The rhythms of her varied expressions are burned into my subconscious like a favorite song from childhood. The familiar tune causes my heart to race, and I rush to sing along with the melody because I know every word.

"You're well on your way to becoming a famous photographer, aren't you?" I say excitedly.

"Maybe!" She crinkles her nose as if she doesn't deserve the accolades.

We sit in silence, waiting for our drinks to arrive. With the exception of my mother and sister, Shay is the only woman whose silence I can share comfortably. I prop my elbow on the edge of the table, lean my head into the palm of my hand. The question of whether I can get Shay back isn't an equation to solve but an expedition to undertake.

The bartender delicately places the two beverages between us, careful to keep steady eye contact with me. Shay and I each pick one up and clink them together. She holds my gaze and raises one eyebrow curiously. She's just like her brother, a quiet mastermind. I wish I knew what she was thinking.

"So have you been playing in any bands or looking for a new singer?" she asks.

"No singer, no new bands, no music. We tried and failed. Nelson and I are just patiently waiting for you and Parker to come back to your senses."

"You should have come with me." She furiously shakes her head back and forth.

"I know. And If I had to make the choice again— between never playing another chord again and you, I'd choose you. One hundred times over, you. When you were gone, there was no music in my life anyway."

I take a long, hard swig and finish my Shultz in three gulps. I demurely look away, suppressing my overwhelming desire to go down on her like the lights go down in a citywide blackout. Then Shay pulls me close to her. Finally, the moment I have been waiting for.

She whispers in my ear, "The man in the booth to our right is paparazzi and he's trying to get a shot of us."

I lean into her, nestle my face in her neck, and whisper back, "Have you ever outrun the paparazzi before?"

I throw some money down on the table, she grabs my hand, and we run, but I crash into a bar stool. We must look like we're high on something, ducking and weaving through an otherwise slow-moving, dimly lit lounge at nearly 2 a.m. Still, it doesn't stop the guy from following us to the front of the lounge. He's yelling out aggressive questions, trying to get our attention: "Taryn, Shay? Where's Nelson? Where's Parker?"

We arrive at the damask wall and have to wait for it to open. Instead of trying to catch up to us, the guy's camera flashes as he yells out, "Is Parker's video true? Are you two on a date?"

Once my vision clears from the flashes, I see the entire front of the lounge staring at us. Our waiter's caught up to the guy harassing us, demands that he delete the photos. The paparazzi guy pushes his black square-framed glasses up on his nose and acquiesces. "Get out, and don't ever come back here," the waiter yells at him.

The damask wall opens and releases Shay and me, but we hear the click-click-click of cameras going off just outside the front door of the speakeasy.

"They're out there. That asshole must have called his stupid paparazzi friends," I say to Shay.

"Are you two all right?" the bouncer asks us. I hear the click-click-click again and I know we can't walk out the front door. The bouncer can't stop people from waiting in front of the place since they're on a city street. We can see them outside the door through the glass windows, cameras in hand, waiting for me and Shay to step outside again. It's only a matter of time before pictures of us end up on everyone's social feeds.

The bouncer asks the young woman in the boa to escort us out the back. As much as Shay loves being behind a camera, she's not the biggest fan of being in front of one. We were usually let off the hook when Parker was around since photographers focused on him most.

The woman with the boa directs us to follow her through a windowless hallway laden with boxes upon boxes of beer and alcohol.

"Don't worry. This happens to us every now and then when we have celebrities trying to hang out low-key. We're well trained in getting you out the back door."

She points to the door we need to go through. "Cross the parking and you'll end up on the other side of Tenth Avenue. Good luck and Happy New Year."

Shay and I exit the bar like criminals fleeing the scene of a bank robbery.

There are many things in my life that I don't understand, but why I love Shay is not one of them. I am and have always been in love with her. Once you fall victim to it, you quickly realize that nothing is more unbearable than being in love.

As we wait under the full, bright moon for a car to pick us up, I look around to check if the coast is clear and pin her against the brick facade of the building next door.

We've kissed each other a hundred times tonight, but only in our minds, with our glances, in the tender touch of our hands. Now, I move my lips to meet hers and our mouths open—but she backs away.

"I'm sorry, Taryn. I'm not ready for this."

Chapter 15

Rest of the World Go By

It's an unseasonably warm night for February in NYC. On the street outside the Brokered Social, an impossibly good-looking avant-garde crowd waits in line to enter. I walk past them and go straight to the hostess, who sits at a booth just inside. She's the one holding The List.

"Welcome to the Brokered Social," the young brunette with Prada leopard-print glasses pipes up when I approach her.

I say, "Taryn Taylor," and she runs her finger down a piece of paper and strikes off my name with a Sharpie. She smiles deferentially as she points me to the main room. "Shay's exhibit is just behind the grand staircase in the next room."

I take in the sleek, modern space, the evidence of the last few years of Shay's hard work and sacrifices hanging from eleven-foot walls. I make my way past the staircase, and when I don't see Shay, I head straight to the bar and pull an already-poured glass of red wine from its row.

Enter four women wearing all black, descending from the central staircase, the last of which is Shay. I lock eyes with her as she comes down slowly, step by step. The three women she's walking with breeze past me nonchalantly, disturbing my peaceful, admiring reverie. Shay breaks off from the group, and the women go over to a piece and spend the requisite time in front of it, and then the next, and the next. I haven't seen this many people wearing all black and searching for ways to make small talk since the last funeral I attended. My hands search for something to do as I wait for Shay to approach me. I scrutinize my drink and think of funny quips to bestow upon her when she finally makes it over to me—if she makes it over. I crane my neck to see if yet another guest has stopped her on her measured and purposeful journey across the room toward me.

Sweat prickles my neck when Shay finally comes up to me. In that moment, the way her eyes sparkle at me melts my heart. I would testify under oath that she's the only woman I have ever loved.

"You look beautiful," I say, hoping my voice carries enough to disrupt anyone else considering breaking her stride and stealing her attention away from me.

Suddenly, it's as if every face in the room were watching me. Perhaps I said it louder than intended. Shay studies my face, laughs, and kisses me hello. "Thank you for coming."

"Thank you for having me."

The faces flicker past us. A wry smile forms on my face when I realize just how much of Shay they want and how little of her I'm going to be able to have tonight.

Shay drags me by the hand and pulls me toward a portrait. "This one is my favorite." She tilts her head from side to side, inspecting the shot in front of us. It's a black and white portrait of a saxophonist with skin as dark as mocha and a humble mustache, lost in what one can only assume is a downbeat solo.

I study it. "It's stunning."

"Thank you." She cracks a tiny smile.

"I mean it, Shay. Your work is gorgeous. I knew you had talent—I just didn't realize you had this much talent."

She moves down a smidge to the next photograph and gently pulls me in a little closer to her. We stand across from it, staring at it together. It's me, under her on the bed, the morning we broke up.

"I wasn't expecting to see this here."

"I lied before." Her hand brushes up against mine and her pinky clasps mine. "This one is my favorite."

Shay turns away from me because someone has just tapped her on the shoulder to introduce her to a woman with high cheekbones and jet black hair—an editor at a magazine? A model?

The gallery fills up around me, people fitting themselves in the spaces between me and Shay that were formerly exposed. I grab another glass of red wine from the bar and walk over to the least crowded corner. The portraits in front of me were taken on the 6 subway. There's a bright-eyed young girl wearing a fur-collared coat, looking part mafia gangster and part dress-up doll. Seeing all these faces lined up in front of me, I can see Shay's naked talent. Lost in the anonymity of a subway ride, maybe even unaware that her camera was trained on them, her subjects allowed themselves to be seen, whether they wanted to be or not. That's what it means to be part of the grit and grace of New York City: you agree to share yourself, your beauty, and your persona with everyone around you, regardless of your mood.

It's funny that just a few years ago, the thought of an event like this would have put Shay in hives. She claimed she was too edgy a photographer for this scene. She thought galleries were too polished. Her time away, in my opinion, seems to have done her some good. She has finally come out of Parker's shadow, out of photographing him while he takes up too much space for her own light to shine through.

I continue to stroll along the perimeter of the room. Her photos tell stories way better than our songs ever have. Her subjects convey moods deeper than any melody we've ever played. In fact, the only thing her photography and our music have in common is that they both benefit from her raw talent.

I'm so lost in thought that I don't even realize that Nelson's arrived. I watch him from afar and then walk closer to him until I'm standing within earshot. He grabs a piece of salmon-encrusted toast off a platter. With the charisma of a late-night talk show host, he's arrested the attention of the group of fellow hipsters surrounding him—"We were mad as a bag of ferrets. We would go to shows in club basements with set times that commenced well after midnight, hoping to become the next big band."

One of the guys listening to Nelson grabs an hors d'oeuvre. His lips smack together as he chews. "Do you miss playing in a band?" he asks him.

Nelson nods and his hair flows side to side. "I do, but"—he looks around and points at a figure in the crowd—"Parker needs to come back!" I turn around to see who he's pointing to, and to my surprise, it's Parker, moving discreetly through the crowd. That this is the first time Parker and I are seeing each other in person since he left the band is proof of how stubborn we both are.

Nelson spots me and excuses himself. He puts his arm in the crook of mine and guides me away from Parker. His walk is like a shot of whiskey, neat and full of purpose. We stand at a tall bar table adorned with nothing but a lit three-wick candle.

"Is this the first time you're seeing him?" He asks.

"Since when, the video? His return from rehab? Since he left the band?"

Nelson's eyes are bright and alert and I can tell by his expression that he knows my answer to all three hypothetical questions is "yes."

"What are you drinking?" he asks.

"House wine." I shrug.

While I wait for Nelson to fetch me another glass of wine, I watch Parker walk across the room. Despite the people flowing back and forth across my line of sight, I keep my eyes trained on him. I am conflicted about whether I should go and talk to him. From my vantage point, I can tell he hasn't spotted me yet.

He paces down the wall, seemingly enjoying the exhibit. He looks about ten pounds lighter than when I last saw him, and he's lost the rosy color I was so used to seeing on his cheeks. I can see from his profile that he's smiling slightly as he studies one of Shay's portraits. Parker searches it very closely, showing more than just polite interest, and as I walk toward him I see him furrow his brow. When I finally come into his peripheral and he notices me, I see that the portrait he's admiring is one of him, onstage at our last show.

Parker and I greet each other.

"It's so nice to *see* you." He moves a few feet back from me.

"Hi." I wave.

Perhaps he is comforted by my simple greeting.

"Hello." He moves in closer, placing his arms around me and gently hugging me.

We hold the embrace for convention's sake until one of us breaks it off.

After all this time, I am unprepared for how to handle Parker. His presence makes me feel uneasy, and maybe that is by design on his part.

Nelson walks back and hands me my wine. He speaks with his glass held up to his mouth as if he were in the CIA.

"How's it going, mate?" Nelson tilts his head toward Parker.

Parker embraces Nelson.

"You're shaping up to be quite the hugger," I joke.

"It's a habit I'm working on, being more emotional," Parker admits.

"Parker," I fire back, "I anxiously await to see how supremely your emotions fuck this night up."

"All right! Taryn!" Nelson cocks his head at me.

I take a small sip and turn to face the growing crowd.

Nelson lets out a bunch of air, outwardly deflated.

Parker speaks softly. "I get why you feel that way, and I promise you, everything is going to be okay."

I turn around to face him again. I can't help but feel charmed by his confidence; despite my anxious outburst, he's radiating coolness and ease.

Parker holds eye contact with me for a moment, smiling. He looks thoughtfully off into the distance, then looks back at me and smiles again.

I stare at him, transfixed, and then I start to laugh hysterically.

"Taryn?" Nelson says.

I just keep laughing and laughing about whether Parker is going to ruin tonight for Shay.

"What's in your wine?" Nelson peers into my drink.

Panic and worry, I think to myself.

"Do you think maybe we can go speak privately?" Parker points toward the second-floor loft. There are very few people on it.

I nod and Nelson waves us off. "Oh, okay, I'm just going to hang back, mates." He waves at us.

We climb countless stairs before finally settling into a corner of the loft. Our presence causes the space to clear out.

"You can see the entire gallery from here." Parker sweeps his arm at the downstairs area.

"Careful," I say, shaking the rather tenuous modern cable railing. We stand side by side, our backs against the wall, overlooking the gallery.

"Parker, why did you put out that video?"

"If you would have asked me six months ago, I wouldn't have been able to tell you."

"Well, it's good that I am asking you today?" I shrug.

"It is, actually. You know, I gave it all up. Drinking, drugs, vaping, all at once, and you know what I miss most?"

"Enlighten me."

"Vaping!"

"Huh, that's surprising."

"But I had to do it."

"Give up vaping?"

"No, I had to get sober. I was a mess."

"Yeah, pretty sure you don't need to confess to me what a mess you were." I shift my weight to face him. "I kind of lived through that madness."

"I missed you. And I made the video to get your attention."

I pull back. "Seriously? That's a bit childish. And yet, the most pointedly honest you've ever been." I place my hands behind me to brace myself against the railing. "I don't know if I should be offended or impressed."

"I thought it would be my pièce de résistance. Turns out I just pissed off a lot of people."

"Yeah, ya did." I laugh.

"Our fans still leave me brutal comments," he presses on.

"As they should." I laugh.

"I did you a favor." He turns his head and looks at me askew. There's something wholly indescribable about the shift in his gaze. "I feel responsible for reconnecting you and Shay again."

"Reconnecting me and Shay," I scoff.

"Yeah. You are here aren't you?"

"Holy shit, Parker. I forgot how narcissistic you are."

"It's true, admit it."

I shift my weight from one side to another. "True or not, you didn't invent everything. You can't take credit for it all, especially me and Shay. Obviously, she and I would have reconnected on our own terms. All you did was further drive a wedge between us all."

"At least I'm consistent." His shoulders collapse.

"Do you need to get back in touch with your emotions or something? You're kind of being a dick."

"I should drop the facade. It's one of my character defects," he confesses reluctantly.

"Character what?"

"Oh, never mind. It's something I've been learning about in recovery. That switch in me when I try to take credit for everything."

"How's that all going? Recovery?"

"Even in rehab where honesty is rare, progress is sketchy, and remorse often nonexistent, I managed to have a moment of clarity."

"I've heard that saying, like in movies and stuff, 'a moment of clarity.'"

"It's usually what you experience just before you land in Alcoholics Anonymous. And I had it. I had my moment of clarity just after that video was released and just before all the die-hard Pause For Effect fans started sending me thinly veiled death threats."

"One or two of those might have been from me." I smirk.

He looks down at the floor, "I deserved it."

"It's time for you and me to let things go, Parker."

"Yes, in my recovery, when I get to Step 9, I'll make amends to people."

"Step 9?"

"Yeah, there are steps. Twelve of them."

"Which one are you on?"

"The third."

"And what's that all about?"

He recites it as if he's reading it from the wall: "Made a decision to turn our will and our lives over to the care of God as we understood him."

"Hmmm, I'm surprised, this sounds religious."

"It's spiritual, not religious. I struggled with that part of it too, but I found a hack that helps me heal in two ways."

"Oh, what's that?"

"God . . . is . . . my mom."

"Oh," I'm taken aback. Not sure whether he intends to come off as someone who's high on something or if that's really what he believes.

Parker's parents had a very hard time conceiving. After five miscarriages, they were close to giving up when they learned that they were pregnant with the fetus now known as Parker. Parker's mother had devoted years of her life to carrying a baby. There was a two-year stretch where she only spent a few months not with child. She had a very easy time becoming pregnant but a hell of a time maintaining it. With Parker, her water broke two months early, and she was on bed rest in the hospital for a month before an infection set in. Parker was delivered via C-section four weeks early and received the best neonatal care. Two months after his birth, he left the neonatal intensive care unit. His mother's infection traveled through her body, and while she was able to see Parker during those first few weeks from outside his Isolette, she didn't make it long enough to hold him in her arms or take him home.

"She's your . . . God?" I am trying with all my might to tread lightly.

"I think of it like—she's more like my angel, she watches over me. And it's helping me heal and deal with much of my addiction related to her loss."

"It's like a two-for-one? Heal and deal?"

He pauses, probably aware that I want so badly to keep wisecracking. "It's my process and it's what's keeping me sober, so it's working for me."

I wave my hands up. "I am so sorry. I might have to join you on that Step 9 now too."

"Well, I'll be on that step someday. I've hurt a lot of people, and you're definitely one of them." He leans back against the wall and puts one foot behind him, arching his back a bit.

"I guess we've all hurt each other," I admit. "I hurt Shay when I didn't leave with her. You hurt us all when you left the band."

He pushes himself off the wall and leans over the landing to point down to Nelson, who is impervious to our conversation. "He's the only one who hasn't hurt any of us."

I lean over the landing too, pushing myself against the thin metal wire railing to catch a glimpse of Nelson. "No, he's never hurt any of us. He's just a victim of all of our bullshit."

I laugh and make to turn around to face Parker, but when I shift my body against the metal wires, the top one snaps. It whips against my leg and I bend over to catch it from snapping against the other, but then I'm falling at a velocity that has my mind racing backward while my body plummets forward. The sense of the fall is immediate— the swiftness and depth of it. No, this isn't a fall from grace or a metaphor for falling in love—I am actually falling backward from the loft, toward the gallery floor below.

The air tears through me like a tornado. It strikes me in the mouth and punches me in the stomach. I bellow and beg for the insentient air to return to my lungs. I gasp. The marriage of my flesh and bones upon the floor means that I can fall no longer. I scramble to sit up. The white noise of chitchat disappears and is replaced by the thumping of my pulse.

They say that in the last moments, you see your whole life flashing before your eyes. But I only register bits of random scenes:

Playing onstage.

Gwen applying my makeup.

Posing for a photo with Nelson.

Holding Shay's hand.

Tuning my guitar.

Signing an autograph.

My father.

Is this what death looks like? My last moment, my last minute, my last second of life? I didn't even get to record a live album. Will I ever have an encore?

• • •

As the room comes back into focus, it feels crooked, like the floor is tilted. I'm lying on my side. My attempts to sit up are futile. The brightening of the light brings with it miscellaneous thoughts.

Suddenly, I'm ten years old again, on a road trip. I stick my head out the window of the car, which is driving seventy-five miles per hour, and my glasses fly off my face and onto the highway. It's like sucking a river through a straw—the air fighting to leave me and the wind struggling to punch it back in. The floor rises with the sole purpose of bringing me to my knees.

I black out for a few seconds and wake up to the muffled feeling of being wheeled on a gurney through the gallery.

"Are you Taryn Taylor?" the EMT asks as he hovers over my body.

"Who's Taryn?" I mutter in a state of disarray.

I blink as I look up at the man's face, blurring out of focus. My life is being threatened in the most absolute way possible: gradually and all at once, And my last thought is . . . Shay . . . I ruined the night for Shay . . .

Chapter 16
Until We Meet Again

"There's a time and a place to die, Taryn. This is not yours." Shay's calmness is both reassuring and terrifying. She's sitting in the chair next to my bed, holding my hand despite the IV that's affixed to it.

I glance around my grand hospital room. I'll bet many a celebrity has recovered from a face-altering surgery in a room this spacious. I make a sorry attempt to sit up, but my chest, heavy as an ocean current, violently forces me back onto the bed. The high-pitched pulsing of my heart monitor is so predictable that it could be used in a techno remix. The room is spiraling out of control. It's worse than any hangover.

"Parker?" I mumble under my breath.

Mom is across the room but somehow hears me. She takes a deep breath. It's similar to the one she took when

I was seven and she had to explain why my goldfish was floating on its side. "He's not back yet."

"Taryn, how are you doing?" Gwen asks with an impatience that suggests she's asked me more than once. When I don't respond, she settles into an oversized blue hospital chair and reapplies her lipstick.

Shay gently moves my hair to the side and kisses me on the forehead.

"Are we in heaven?" I ask.

"No, sweetie, we're at Weill Cornell." She squeezes my hand.

"She's becoming more lucid at least." Gwen furrows her brow. "Her painkillers must be on point."

Through half-closed eyelids, I watch Gwen smile at her own reflection in the large window.

Mom searches frantically through her bag for money. "I don't have cash to tip the nurses!" she announces as if she's shouting out an answer on *Family Feud*. Turning up empty, she sifts, in a last-ditch effort, through the pockets of her jeans.

"Mom, they aren't delivering pizza. You don't tip them." Gwen pulls an old receipt from her bag. After unfolding it and exploring its mysteries, she flips it over and presses her ruby-rose lipstick to it. Then she crumples it up and throws it on my abandoned tray table. It lands on the plastic serving dish between the unopened applesauce and the untouched bread.

Mom thinks it's customary to tip the nurses. How I wish I could muster up the energy to laugh at her, but I am half-asleep, somewhere between the stars and the ocean. If not for my unfortunate state, I would be carrying on with them in my own unique and ridiculous way. Being on the receiving end of their dysfunctional coping methods is much less fun. I am the one lying in a hospital bed, staring at stark white walls that stretch to infinity—and when Mom tells me she just went to the pharmacy, I ask her if that's a new nightclub. My mind digs up non-sequitur memories of Shay's exhibition. In flashes, I remember the portraits I saw, so gorgeous. The pillow crackles as I slowly lift my head.

"I can have lunch delivered to them," Mom says as she taps her foot apprehensively.

"Mom, that is totally unnecessary." Gwen is really good at assuaging other people's guilt, especially if it helps her avoid doing work she doesn't want to do.

"I can call Nelson and have him pick up lunch on the way." Shay offers.

"Abso-fucking-lutely not, Shay!" Gwen snaps her compact shut and throws it into her bag.

"What's this I hear about soddy lunch?" Nelson calls out as he slinks through the door.

"*Bloody bollocks.*" Gwen mimics Nelson's accent under her breath.

Ignoring their squabbles, Shay moves up to me and offers me a concerned frown. "Hey," she whispers softly.

"Why does everyone keep kissing me on the forehead?" I whisper back.

"Darling, you fell from a loft." Shay is kind and even-keeled but Gwen barrels in to interrupt her.

"You're on so many painkillers, you probably can't even feel the pain you're in."

Nelson takes a moment to contemplate where to sit. Eventually, he chooses the edge of my bed. I look around and notice the different machines beeping around me.

My vision swirls. Shay's face blurs. The last thing I see before falling asleep is a drop of liquid making its way down the waterslide of my IV.

• • •

I make out various circular shapes looming over me, ranging in size from large to small like a model solar system. When my eyes focus, it turns out that the shapes aren't planets but faces. As the beeping continues around me, I look around at the people lounging in my hospital room. My bed, comprised mostly of air, puffs up and decompresses in a rhythmic cacophony that makes about as much sense as a Limp Bizkit song.

Gwen stands, yawns, and offers her seat to Shay. Her kind gesture is a cover-up that allows her to succumb to her overwhelming compulsion to rearrange the flower bouquet. Spend as much time with your sibling as I do with mine and you can spot her tics and triggers and sometimes even predict her actions.

Picking up my iPhone, I glance at my alerts: I have one hundred-plus unread text messages; my name has been tagged on all of my social feeds. Disregarding this, I place my phone on the end table and finally ask, "Should we talk about what happened?"

Shay reaches out to hold my hand, offering me a reassuring smile.

Mom answers quickly, as if she's been rehearsing her response—"I promise we'll talk at home, in a comfortable and safe environment."

A nurse enters the room, and from the ID tag that hangs from her peach-colored lanyard, I deduce that her name is Eliza. "How are you feeling?" Eliza asks as she rips the Velcro from my arm. She marks my blood pressure on her mobile cart.

"Why does my bed fill up with air and decompress every few minutes?"

Eliza laughs. "That feature is for people who are here long-term. It's so your legs don't atrophy. I think we can turn that off." She reaches behind me and flips a switch. The mattress fills up, and once firm, the white noise of constantly moving air ceases.

"Miss Taylor, her numbers are good," she says to Mom while shining an obnoxiously bright light in my eyes. She moves to check on my bandages. Just as I'm about to ask her the extent of my injuries, the door bangs open. Eliza clicks the light off.

Parker blows into the room. I push myself up in bed and notice the trees just outside my ground-floor window. The rustling of branches in the barren trees tells me that there's a breeze. Just behind them, the sun is beginning to set, obscuring the paparazzi that Parker inadvertently brought with him. The photographers are jockeying with each other, trying to get *the shot*—the one the press will pay good money for. Gwen sees me peering out of the window and goes to close the blinds to provide a modicum of privacy.

Parker walks up to me, leans in and wraps his arm around me. "Honey, how are you feeling?"

I shrink back from him a little. "This is all your fault."

He clutches the fictitious pearls that he's not wearing. "My fault?!"

"Not now!" Mom scolds us both.

Once Parker moves away from me, Gwen swoops to my side and says, "I know this is going to sound insensitive and possibly even cruel, but . . ."

"What's going to sound cruel?" I whine, not in the mood for more bad news.

"Well, the paparazzi are outside . . . . I should do your makeup." She moves the plastic serving dish onto the end table, and from her bag she lays out her makeup brushes piece by piece, like an artist in front of a blank canvas.

Mom comes to my defense. "You are not doing her makeup, honey."

"Yeah, Gwen, you're being absurd," I say to her.

Gwen hovers over me and holds a compact mirror to my face. The right side of my face looks like it fought Mike Tyson in his prime. I raise my hand and feel the fire that emanates from it.

Gwen packs her tools back into her bag. "Here—" She throws lip gloss onto my bed. "At least use this."

"Taryn," Shay puts in, "I'm parked in the basement. I can take you out through the garage and bring you home."

We are interrupted by a tall white man with a football player's build, who has just entered. His presence dissolves the push-and-pull between me and Mom and Gwen. "Hello, I'm Dr. Sullivan."

"And I'm Parker," Parker calls out from the corner.

Dr. Sullivan notices that it is, in fact, Parker. He regains his composure by glancing down at his iPad. He grabs the chair that Gwen abandoned, but just as he is about to sit, he does the thing that people do when they see Parker.

"You're . . ." He coughs. "Well, you're Parker."

Parker points his index finger at the doctor, tilting it down at an angle. "The one and only."

Dr. Sullivan looks around the room, trying to make sense of this merry band of misfits that includes his patient and her defunct band.

"Taryn, I'm the doctor on call tonight—I mean today, I've been here since midnight—and I hear that you're being released today. I need to ask you some questions, and I apologize if you've heard them before. I understand you had a pretty big fall last night?"

"I fell from the loft."

"How—" Dr. Sullivan pauses, "did you fall?"

"The metal railing wires became detached—I'm not really sure how."

Dr. Sullivan glances at his iPad and back at me. "It looks like . . ." He swipes left several times as if rejecting potential dates on a hookup app. "Can you tell me the last thing you remember about the fall?"

"I remember—" As I nervously scan my memory, I survey the faces of everyone in the room. A wave of confusion passes through me as images from the exhibit flash through my mind like a time-lapse video.

Dr. Sullivan pulls his chair a little closer to me.

"I remember the fall," I say. "The gallery. And the ambulance ride here?" I finish as if asking him a question. "*I am so sorry,*" I mouth to Shay.

"*It's fine,*" she mouths back, waving me off.

"Did I ruin the night?"

"You just had to make it all about you," Shay jokingly quips.

"Oh, Shay's fine!" Parker guffaws. "There wasn't a photograph left on the wall to sell."

"Oh stop, Parker," she exclaims.

"It's true. You left with Taryn. There wasn't one portrait that didn't have someone staking a claim to it—tell her." He motions to Nelson.

"It's true," Nelson nods. "Sadly, people weren't sure if Taryn would make it and—" Nelson pauses, "the scene got real dark, real fast. Savages." He shakes his head. "Those people are savages."

"Well, that sounds like an interesting story," Dr. Sullivan interrupts. "Okay, good. Well, the good news is . . ." He looks around the room. "How old are you?" he asks me.

"Twenty-three."

"You're young. You'll heal fast." He waves his right hand in the air.

"What's the good news?"

"Oh, right—the good news is that you can definitely go home today." He has a slight tic, which causes him to squint his eyes every few seconds. At first, I thought he was winking at me.

"What's the prognosis, doc?" Parker looks up from his phone.

Dr. Sullivan looks at Mom and she smiles, granting him permission to humor Parker.

"Well, she's very lucky, no concussion. We've given her some pain medicine for the bruises and cuts, but other than that, she's going to be fine." He shifts his gaze from Parker and back to me.

"That's great news." Parker looks back down at his phone, smiles, and taps his finger twice on the screen.

"However—" The doctor puts his hand on my arm and squints his left eye twice. "I am going to have you leave in a wheelchair, and you'll do some follow-up visits over the next few months to make sure everything stays copacetic."

"Live in a wheelchair!" Parker throws his hands up in the air. "She's paralyzed?"

"Leave." Nelson corrects him in a tone as measured as the ingredients of apple pie. "She will have to *leave* in a wheelchair, mate."

"Parker, have you told everyone what we were talking about up there?"

Everyone but the doctor turns their eyes away from me and says nothing. It's not their silence that puts my stomach in knots; it's the truth that lies behind it. Dr. Sullivan looks at Mom, who nods, confirming that my hysterical outburst is normal and not at all related to the fall.

Parker sits down and crosses one leg over the other. He suddenly grins. "Taryn and I were having a moment of reconciliation, one might call it." He makes exaggerated puppy dog faces at Nelson and Shay. They just stare at him and then back at me, not really understanding what led him to making this big a declaration.

"Well, it sounds like we're all caught up here." Dr. Sullivan draws away from my bedside.

"Am I allowed to get dressed now?" I ask, speaking to no one and everyone at the same time. My entire body feels battered and tired. A migraine has started to manifest, thrumming away achingly.

Nelson gets up from the end of my bed and helps me to my feet. Gwen follows me into the bathroom just like she did when we were kids. She sits on the toilet and watches as I become reacquainted with my reflection. The oil buildup from missed shower has added shine instead of grit to my hair. I flip it from side to side and then realize that the swift motion is making the thumping in my skull worse.

"He seems different since he got back from rehab," says Gwen, verbalizing what I already know.

I bite my bottom lip and stare back at myself in the mirror. "Makeup would never help this face, Gwen."

"It's all superficial. You'll look fine in a week." She turns my face to the side. "Ten days, tops."

"What's in the bag?"

Gwen begins to unzip her Coach weekender. The zipper gets stuck due to her overpacking. When you travel with Gwen, you can give up on hoping to board a flight with just carry-ons. Inevitably, a member of the in-flight crew will scream those dreaded five words: "I need a pink tag."

Gwen wiggles the zipper a bit and it comes unstuck. She pulls out my black yoga pants, an oversized gray hoodie, black running shoes, a Brooklyn Nets snapback cap, and a black scarf big enough to swaddle a small child.

"Gwen," I say.

"Yes?" She lays everything out on the counter.

My eyes dart to the scarf and back at her.

"What? It's cold out."

We emerge from the bathroom. Gwen comes out the same person she was when she went in. I come out a sporty snow person. Three slow, dangerous steps later, I remove the ridiculous hat and scarf.

Dr. Sullivan nods at me and swiftly pulls the IV out. I am finally free. The others run around the room, gathering their belongings as if they'd missed their hotel's wake-up call and were late for a flight. I am the final item collected. Dr. Sullivan and his massive muscles gently place me into a wheelchair.

Dr. Sullivan says to Parker in a hushed tone, "My teenage daughter is a huge fan."

Parker snaps a selfie with Dr. Sullivan. "Tell your daughter to look at my Instagram later," Parker says. "She'll be very proud of dear old Dad."

Mom wheels me out of the room and stops at the nurses' stations to thank them.

Gwen whispers out of the side of her mouth, "Hide me from that guy in the scrubs!" She tips her head down as she kneels in front of me.

"What?" I look conspicuously around the hallway, twisting my neck as far as I can. "Gwen, they're all in scrubs."

"I had a one-night stand with him."

"You aren't half drunk in kitten heels," I say. "He won't recognize you."

"I'll take her from here." Shay grabs the handlebars and wheels me forward. She puts my bag in my lap and I unzip it, take a peek in. It's still there, my journal.

Parker heads out the front door with Nelson, Gwen, and Mom in tow. The sun drops behind the horizon, draping the remaining paparazzi in a grayish hue. Gwen is hiding between Parker and Nelson. Maybe she should've taken the scarf and hat. I faintly hear the paparazzi calling, "Parker! Nelson! Shay! Taryn!" The elevator doors open and Shay wheels me in. She leans over me and presses the button for parking level B1.

As the doors close, Shay turns to me, kneeling down, and asks the one question everyone else neglected to ask. "Did you two really make up?"

"Sure did." I laugh.

"Good on you." Shay laughs too. "How do you feel?"

"Well," I start, "I feel like I'm broken."

"There's only one part of you that's broken, Taryn, and that's your spirit."

"I can't believe I didn't even break a bone. It feels like the whole thing happened for nothing."

"Everything has a purpose, even life's tragedies."

"What about you?" I ask. "Are you okay?"

She smiles softly and strokes my face gently with her thumb. "I'm okay now that I know you're okay." Her voice is low, imbued with emotions that I can't quite place. But I can see the love shimmering softly in her eyes.

The elevator doors open slowly and Shay wheels me out. She hits the remote on her key chain and the trunk of her car opens automatically. I start to get out of the wheelchair on my own, but she grabs my arm.

"It's okay," I tell her. "If I'm going to heal, I have to start somewhere."

Shay folds the wheelchair and places it in the trunk. "I have strict orders to join you at your mother's," she calls as I walk toward the passenger side of the car.

She runs over to hold the door open for me. When I am secured, she closes the door and jogs briskly to the driver's side. I wait for her to get in and offer her a smile.

I look in the side mirror and see the wheelchair return area.

"Shay." I look directly at her.

She turns her head to me. "Taryn." She adds, "Listen, Taryn?"

"Yes?"

She pauses, her eyes flitting across my face, "You can't . . . you can't ever do that again."

"Fall from a balcony?" I ask.

"Yes but also . . ." She's trying to come up with the words. "Seeing you that vulnerable . . . I felt really helpless just watching you fall and lie there like that. For a few moments, I was so sure that you were gone. That I had lost you."

I take her hand to offer some comfort as she speaks.

"Taryn, I don't want to make it about me obviously, but I'm just telling you what I felt and what I saw. I never want to see you in such a vulnerable state again."

"It's all right now, Shay." I stroke her hand. "I am all right."

She nods, her eyes glinting with unshed tears. "We'll be all right."

"Let's go home?" I suggest, letting her hand go.

The parking attendant raises the gate for us to exit, and we wave to thank him.

"Shay, I don't think you're supposed to leave the hospital with the wheelchair in tow."

"I just stole a wheelchair?"

"You totally just stole a wheelchair."

I laugh even though it causes every bruise on my body to make its presence known.

"I think we can keep it now." She laughs.

Shay's hand falls onto mine on the center console. She looks down at our hands gently touching, and for a second neither one of us shifts position. Despite hurting all over from the fall, when Shay's hand lands on top of mine, the pain feels less acute.

Chapter 17
Tin Roof Rusted

It's broad daylight when I wake up at my mom's house bleary-eyed. I sit up in bed, staring confusedly at the sunshine pouring through the window, but can't stay in this position for very long. My eyelids grow heavy and the wakefulness ebbs away. I slump back down into a lying position and doze off.

Awake again—I slowly turn over so that my pillow fills the weak space between my neck and head.

When I wake up once more, moments or maybe hours later, I try to cautiously flip over onto my left side. I wasn't prepared for the strength I'd need to pull the blankets up to my chin. I burrow deeper into my pillow and find a comfortable spot in which to settle that doesn't agitate a bruise or cause a shooting pain. My body is finally relaxed, so at ease that I'm finally able to rest my head. But my thought drifts to the peculiar and the bizarre.

In my dream, I am with my father and I am older than I ever was when he was alive, maybe seven or eight years old.

I accompany him to our local music shop. I know he is about to go on tour, and even though we live just uptown and he'll be back home very soon, I insist on joining him to the store.

I silently slip away from my father and wander bravely into an entire row of guitars. I do not understand, of course, that rummaging through the maze of instruments just to pluck the strings of each guitar is wrong.

Now I'm nestled on a veritable island amid the over-stuffed aisles filled wall to wall with musical instruments. Underneath the tower of amplifiers where only a child would look to hide.

He's taking forever, pounding away at a keyboard, not paying any attention to me climbing underneath the stools and up the mountain of amplifiers. I make my way to the top, where—if I could just reach it—I glimpse the ash body and maple neck of the guitar crookedly displayed on the wall.

I grab at the guitar in an effort to bring it down to my level. I envision dragging it across the store, leaning against the wall and staring unblinkingly into the eyes of the customers (my new fans) as I twang the strings.

I ignore the frantic cries of my father, the handful of strangers calling out my name to help him find me, until the frenzy of everyone pitching in finds me holed up in a corner with an instrument double my size.

I watch my father's face pass from relief to annoyance to bewilderment all in a moment as he tries to work out how I have managed to sneak away from him and carry this guitar across the place. He starts and stops several times before finally settling on, "Taryn, honey, what fierce strength you have when you want something."

Later, after he pays at the cash register, we walk out to the middle of Times Square. My father sits me down on a bench, puts his arm around me, tells me he's very proud of me.

"You're not mad?" I ask. Afraid I've done something very wrong.

"I was a little scared," he admits, "when I thought you were missing."

"But you aren't mad?" I ask again.

"No, honey. I'm not mad at you."

"Dad," I say to him as I crawl out from under his arm, "can I come with you? On tour and play music?"

He looks out upon Times Square, with its millions of dazzling and dancing lights.

"Sweetie, I am so impressed with who you are, and I see the big girl you're going to be when you grow up."

"Will I have my own guitar, Dad?"

"You'll have so many that you'll need a whole room to store them all."

"But I want one now," I plead.

My father leans back on the bench, stares up to the sky. And then bolts up as if by inspiration, saying, "When I get back from tour, we'll go back to the store and pick out a guitar of your very own."

"In any color I want?" I say excitedly.

"In any color you want, darling," he says.

The scene shifts to my mother and I, waiting at the door, receiving the news of his passing. My father never came home from that tour.

"There is so much I need to say to you." The words slip from my lips to my father.

Abruptly, I open my eyelids and the room comes into focus. I turn stiffly to see Shay, lying in the twin bed on the opposite side of the room, her face slack but awake.

"Good morning," I say through my hazy gaze.

"Morning." She wipes her eyes.

"I just had the craziest dream."

"It wasn't a dream. You actually fell from the loft at my exhibit."

I laugh, and even that hurts. "No, that wasn't it. It was about my father."

"Oh yeah?"

"It must be the energy of his stuff—" I nod toward the closet that houses his trunk. "It must be seeping into my subconscious."

"Yeah, that or the painkillers." Shay giggles a little.

"I wish you could have slept in bed with me last night."

"I do too."

"If you're very careful and don't press into any of my bruises, I think we can cuddle."

My request hangs in the air as she struggles to untangle herself from her sheets. She carefully crawls into bed and meticulously engulfs me in her embrace. I fit inside Shay's arms like a Russian nesting doll. This was the kind of lover I've always wanted in Shay, but she knew better—it wasn't the right time for us. Our love then was something that erupted into an uncontrollable blaze, but what I wanted was this, a passion of embers that will burn slow and long, possibly forever.

She asks permission before kissing me on my neck. Though I feel as if I fell from a tree, hitting every branch on my way down limb by limb, being this close to Shay heals me. The warmth of her embrace soothes me in a way that no pain meds can. She's careful not to move, afraid to hurt me with even the slightest infraction, and though she lies nearly statue still, the pulsating energy of being this close to her again energizes me to a point of feeling as if I didn't fall at all.

We stay still for what feels like a lifetime until she sits up. "I'm so afraid I'm going to hurt you." I shift over to my side and look up at her through sleepy eyes. "You won't, I promise."

She smiles at me. "In that case . . ." She gives me a sharp, knowing smile before she drops to her knees and leans over the side of the bed. She kisses me with a ravenous mouth. A calmness within me mixes with a sense of panic, the type you feel when you abruptly awaken from a deep sleep and it takes you a few seconds to get your bearings.

My mind ruminates. "We haven't been in this bed together since high school."

"What is meant to be yours will always find its way to you." Her face is so close to mine that when she closes her eyes, I feel her lashes tickle my cheek. I want to joke, to tell her that her quip sounds like something you'd read in a fortune cookie, but I don't have the energy to muster up my sarcastic humor—and I happen to agree with her: what is meant to be always will be.

"I have a confession." She rubs her fingers against my arm slowly.

"Consider me your priestess." I grasp her fingers with mine.

"I have never been so scared as when I saw you fall." She lowers her voice just a decibel. "There was a shift in me, a change." She very gently puts her hand up to straighten an errant hair caught in my eyelashes. "To witness someone you love"—her voice cracks a little—"and to be unable to stop it from happening." She wipes several tears as they roll down her cheeks.

I feel myself completely unraveling as each word leaves her mouth.

"I love—" she says.

"I love you too," I interrupt.

"No, damn it, Taryn, let me finish."

She's still half on the floor, half leaning onto the bed. I ease myself more onto my side to face her, a bit perplexed by her honesty. A string of moments passes without any words being exchanged, only glances.

Shay tries to get back to the point. "When I realized I could lose you—" She wipes another tear that has fallen down her face. "Two truths crystallized for me. The first is how much I love you." She shifts her weight to one side so that she's resting against the side of the bed. "And the other is that I never want to be without you again."

I move closer to the edge of the bed as if to assert that we belong together—to press my body into hers no matter the physical pain it causes me—to dissolve any space between us, so we become one.

Her lips touch my ear. "I love you," she repeats.

"I love you too," I answer without hesitation. We stay in an embrace for a while longer, basking in each other's company, then Shay stands up.

I ease myself up in my childhood bed. Shay helps me to my feet, cautious not to move me too quickly, and she walks with me downstairs.

• • •

From the first floor bay window, I can not only see Mr. Kelsey riding his snowblower, but hear him too. Gwen, for sure, knows better than to park in front of his house. When she pulls up and zips right into the driveway, he nearly pummels her car with snow.

Mom's heels scrape across the wooden floor and she greets Gwen at the front door. When Mom sees Bradley there too, she immediately begins to fluff the pillows on the couch.

"Heyo," Gwen calls out. The opening of the front door brings a chill gust of wind.

Neo the bird squawks, *"Olá,"* nearly a dozen times.

Gwen asks if she can hug me with the universal arms-in-a-half-circle formation.

"Gently, very gently," I tell her.

"Are you still in a lot of pain?"

"Yes, but the pain meds are really helping." I make a whooshing motion with my head.

Gwen is meticulously put together today: her hair tightly pulled into a neat bun, her fingernails freshly painted deep scarlet red, a white oversized sweater setting off her newly acquired pearl necklace.

"Taryn, I'm sure you remember Bradley."

He looks me over long enough for me to compose a status update, delete it, recompose it, and delete it again.

"I'm so happy to see that you're okay," he says from a safe distance of about four feet away.

"And this is my mom, Marge," Gwen says, turning Bradley to face our mother, who is now collecting books from around the room and placing them in a neat pile on her desk.

Mom's voice competes with that of Neo, who belts out, *"Rauuuuuuur! Boa tarde!"*

"Don't mind the squawks," I warn Bradley. "That's just her bird."

"Hello, Bradley," Mom says as she finally puts everything in her hands down and stops running around the room. "I hope you won't judge me too harshly by my messy home. As you can imagine, I had no idea the girls would both be here this weekend, and I certainly didn't know I would be meeting you."

"Miss Taylor, it's so nice to meet you." He holds out his hand to shake hers.

Gwen interrupts the exchange: "Women." She looks at Mom. "Not girls."

"Yes, Gwen, sorry. You are women. And one day, when you have children of your own, you'll see that they'll always be your girls. Or boys. Or whatever they identify as."

Bradley sits next to Gwen and she instantly melts into him, probably without even realizing it.

Shay walks out to join us all. "Hello!" She waves, unsure of how to react to Bradley.

Gwen's face lights up like a Christmas tree. "Shay!" she hollers with glee. "This is Bradley."

Shay and Bradley glance at each other. "Hi!" Shay walks across the living room with her hand extended. "I'm Shay."

They exchange niceties, and Mom calls out from the kitchen, "Kids, who wants brunch?"

"I would love some," Gwen pops up.

Bradley waits for us to head toward the kitchen.

Mom's boiling water on the stovetop for the French press. She turns to face us as we seat ourselves side by side around the kitchen's center island.

"Bradley! So tell me about yourself." Mom speaks to Bradley in a high-pitched tone.

"Oh sure, ma'am."

Gwen places her hand on Bradley's leg. "I promise you, you don't have to be that formal in this family."

Mom nods to acknowledge that Gwen is right.

"Okay, Miss Taylor. Well, I'm a motocross rider."

"Yes, that sounds exhilarating." Mom sets down four place mats, one in front of each of us. "And do you live around here?" Her motions make her look like a diner waitress doling out plates and silverware.

"In Manhattan, yes." He flattens out the napkin in front of him.

Mom smiles. "And your parents, what do they do?"

I am indefatigable in my attempt to change the subject. I try to lock eyes with Mom but she's looking at Bradley—I raise my glass, motioning for coffee—and I finally just interrupt her: "Mom, may I have some French toast?"

Shay cuts in, "Marge, I would love some too."

Gwen throws a grateful look my way and pipes up, "Mom, I think I mentioned to you the loss Bradley suffered."

"Bradley," Mom walks around the island and puts her arm on his shoulder, "I am so sorry. I hope you don't find me crass."

"It's okay, Miss Taylor, it's true." He winces. "Both my parents have passed." There are two possible reasons for Bradley's swift response. Either the death of his parents feels remote and he'd rather not discuss it—or their passing still means everything to him.

Mom shakes her head slowly. "I am so sorry. You know, we Taylors know a lot about loss.

The room stands still. Bradley hides himself in the confusion of the moment. Then he pivots toward me and makes a heartfelt confession—not about his parents, but about me: "Taryn, I can't tell you how afraid I was when Gwen told me. I was up in Canada yesterday, and when your sister told me I got on a plane."

"Bradley," I say, touching his shiny bald head, "that probably won you major points with Gwen."

Shay smiles a brilliant smile.

"Oh, shut up," Gwen retorts. "He is a nice person, you know."

I turn to Gwen with some difficulty. "Hopefully, you won't influence him otherwise."

"Ha-ha," she mock-snickers. "He was coming home anyway."

"Oh, you couldn't let me have that one?" Bradley laughs.

"I don't want them thinking you're *that* sweet." Gwen kisses him on the cheek.

The tea kettle wails its loud siren and Mom pours the hot water into the French press.

"It's true, actually," Mom says. "I once read a study about how much influence a partner can have on your behavior."

Mom rests the French press right beside her Garland stove. On the shelf just above the range sits a pair of Princess Diana and Prince Charles salt and pepper shakers that are "for show," Mom always says.

"How are you feeling?" Bradley asks.

"My body feels like it's eight hundred shades of fucked up, and I'm currently trying to get it down to a few."

His laugh is hearty and authentic. It doesn't take long before he asks Gwen, "You must have freaked out?"

"She rushed to be at my side in the hospital." I pull myself closer to the island. "The minute she finished her makeup." I laugh a little.

Mom grabs the cinnamon, milk, and eggs. Two clicks and the flame under the griddle swooshes. "Cast iron is a versatile workhorse," she says to the griddle.

When Gwen and I fully extricated ourselves from the house, Mom suffered empty nest syndrome. "Empty nest syndrome is not a clinical condition," she told me as she sobbed over the phone. She decided to gut renovate the kitchen and went full-on Julia Child. She had the cabinets painted Tiffany blue. Books (both Julia's and Jacques') snuggle together to fill the gaps of counter space between the coffee maker and the cutting board. Her KitchenAid mixer is two stops from the sink, "just like Julia's was." The first time she proudly invited Gwen and I after we had moved out (to witness her midlife crisis firsthand), she told us, "My wall oven doesn't squeak." As if it was a concern keeping us up at night.

Mom flips a piece of French toast and then another. The smell of cinnamon and butter wafts through the room.

I take a sip of coffee.

Mom places a plate in front of each of us. "Completely organic French toast. Bon appétit."

Bradley takes the plate Mom offers to him. "This looks delicious."

Mom turns to open the cabinet. "Syrup?" she offers.

"I would love some," Shay says.

"Rauuuurrr!" Neo calls out.

Having a talking bird is, oddly and indirectly, one of my earliest posthumous memories of my father. Our first bird, Princess Saint Lovely, would repeat, "Timothy Taylor and the Standards!" At four years old, the sound of my dead father's name being hurled at me made me act out, but as I got older, I got tired of my fits. With the passage of time, I tired of talking birds as well.

"So, you like riding a bike for a living?" Shay asks Bradley.

"Love it!" He holds his hand in front of his mouth to conceal any food in his teeth.

Gwen moves her French toast around her plate, sopping up puddles of butter on the edges. Then she abruptly drops her fork and bolts.

My instinct is to chase her, but the best I can do is a steady dash behind her into the bathroom.

She's just finished vomiting and sits down on the floor. I close the door behind me and sit down on the ledge of the bathtub, which proves impossibly uncomfortable. As I hoist myself onto the floor to join her, I let out noises generally reserved for those much older than me. I pull out what's left of the toilet paper from its roll and hand it to her. She wipes her mouth with a tiny jagged square.

She looks up at me as if sharing a secret. An important secret that means a lot to her. Do you remember that poetry thing I did . . . ?"

The faded look on Gwen's face is wildly alarming. I remember that night—how could I ever forget that night? It was a doozy of a night filled with many firsts. Gwen speaking in public, her very public confession at a slam poetry competition.

"Yes, Gwen, of course I remember that night. You told me you had an abortion by way of participating in a slam poetry set. One does not simply forget a night like that."

The bathroom tiles are cold, and I shift more than once to try and hit on a comfortable position while Gwen looks off into the distance. "I wanted so badly to have a baby, but the guy I was seeing was just such a loser." She shakes her head.

"What was his name again?"

She shrugs. "His name isn't important, but what does matter is the promise I made to myself, and I promised myself if I ever fell in love again—"

"Hold the fucking phone!" I exclaim. "Are you—?" I point to her midsection. To her completely non-existent bump, perfectly concealed under her chunky sweater.

"Taryn," she says, looking down. "I'm seventeen weeks pregnant."

My eyes widen, my throat opens, I nearly scream, but Gwen cuts me off: "Shut up! No one knows."

"Mom doesn't know?"

"Mom doesn't know." She shakes her head.

"I am so confused. How—how the fuck have you hidden this from us? I feel so . . . stupid. No, betrayed. How?"

"I mean, I know you like women and all, but I don't think I need to explain *how* to you at this age."

"But, seventeen weeks is like—are you like halfway done?" My brain is nearing the brink of explosion, trying to do math without a calculator app.

"We figured it out, and it must have been one of the first nights I met him."

"It's him? Bradley?"

She nods her head.

"But that night at Chloe's, you were drinking! Gwen, you know you can't drink, right?!"

She rolls her eyes. "I wasn't, actually. I had a club soda."

"Holy shit." I cover my mouth, playing the last few months over my mind, trying to catch her in a lie. Has she really not had alcohol? Has she really been contouring her face this fiercely and I just haven't noticed?

"But your morning sickness, I would've noticed that," I stammer.

"You wouldn't have, my sickness just started. Usually this is when it's ending, but for me, for some reason, it's just starting."

"Is it every morning?"

" 'Morning' is a misnomer. You can literally vomit at any hour of the day."

"Holy shit." I tilt my head back and it taps the wall, a motion that reminds me that I'm probably due for a pain-killer—and yet I slightly recoil at the thought. "I'm going to be an aunt." I have to be the best version of myself for this baby.

"It's refreshing that it's only been three minutes and you've already figured out how to make this baby about you."

"Oh, right, yes, back to you."

"I want to be just like one of those cool moms who dresses her kid in trendy clothes, nothing with a Disney character on it, but cool jeans and tiny Adidas. I'll wear nothing but yoga pants, not for style but because I'm actually just coming from a yoga class. I want to be confident enough to breastfeed in public, and then when the baby is old enough to eat, feed it homemade kale and sweet potato chips."

"It sounds like you've given this a lot of thought."

"I have." Gwen steadies herself and rises from the cold floor to wash her hands.

"Does Bradley know?"

"He's known since I've known."

"So is he ready for this? And what type of father does Bradley want to be? What if he's not into organic sweet potato and kale chips?"

"He'll be on board with whatever I want." Gwen smiles wide and flicks water from her fingers onto my face.

"How could you keep this from me?" I wipe the water off of my face with my sleeve.

"Honestly, you were so preoccupied you didn't ever ask how I was doing and I just let you have your drama. I knew I would tell you eventually."

It's hard to know when to stop being pissed at her for not telling me but Bradley knocks on the bathroom door, resolving that problem for me.

"You two okay in there?" he asks through the door.

I raise my arm up and pull on the door handle. The door slightly ajar, he peeks his head in.

"You can come in," Gwen offers.

Bradley sits on the edge of the bathtub next to her. He reaches over and offers me his hand. I grab his and pull myself up—"Ah, ah, ah, movement hurts."

Shay knocks on the door next.

"Come in," the three of us say in unison.

"Marge sent me in. Is everything okay?"

"We should go back out," Gwen directs us.

We join Mom back in the kitchen.

The gravity of the moment eclipses my better judgment and I just blurt out, "While I have you all gathered here"—I grab Shay's hand and hold it in mine—"I want you to hear from me"—glaring at Gwen—"that Shay and I are back together."

"Not now!" Shay shakes her head.

Gwen snaps, "I think I speak for everyone in the room when I say, what the fuck, Taryn?"

Not the reaction I was expecting from Gwen, but okay. Bradley offers a thumbs up, and my mother just continues to look at Gwen.

"Don't you have something you want to say, Gwen?" I mumble under my breath.

"Well," Mom says, "are you going to tell me, or shall I guess?"

Silence falls upon all of us.

And in a tug of war between inappropriate laughter and self-regulation, Gwen's nervous giggle erupts from her throat, lingering long enough to confirm Mom's suspicion before it is quickly arrested. "Mom, I know this might be a bit of a shock, being that you've just met him—" Gwen straightens her necklace. "Bradley and I have decided to have a child together."

And Mom's response is pretty spot on for Mom. She doesn't focus on the news that Gwen is pregnant, but instead on the unborn child's numerology profile, asking, "When did you conceive?" She doesn't wait for a response before turning to Bradley. She doesn't look at him with concern about how well we really know him or whether he'll be a good partner for Gwen, or a good father. She simply says, "And Bradley, what's your sign?"

Gwen shoots Mom a slightly distorted look, and all I can do is laugh at my mom's faith in astrology.

Mom turns back to Gwen. "Honey, I'm your mother. Of course I knew you were pregnant.

"You knew?" I guffaw.

"I'm her mother, of course I did."

"Am I the last to know?"

"Taryn, you've never been pregnant but when you are one day you'll know the signs. And you'll also know that it's a very personal decision when you decide to tell people."

I can't help but look at Shay and smile. Having children one day was a bit of a controversial topic and now when I hear mom say it about me so matter of factly, I share a moment with Shay, acknowledging that that's what our future holds.

"Now, I still want to do a numerology chart." Mom says to Gwen.

I incline my head toward Bradley and whisper. "So . . . yeah . . . Welcome to our crazy family."

Chapter 18
Fascinating Rhythm

What do children, Adele, birthdays, and Pause For Effect's contract with Four Chords Music have in common? They're all highly valued by some people and deemed totally worthless by others.

I stayed up way later than I should have last night discussing everything with Shay—from Gwen's news to someday having children of our own. A conversation of that magnitude might have once triggered a flight or fight reaction in me, but it all felt exactly right against the backdrop of my life's recent reprioritization. My fall from the loft may feel like a punch in the gut, but instead of keeping me down, it's motivated me to grow up. And when Shay and I woke up this morning, and even after lunch, we continued the conversation about *us*. In all essential respects, our beautiful obsession for each other remains unchanged.

Shay's anxiously mentioned the black sky more than once as she paces around the living room.

My excitement is muted but present. I glance at my phone: 5:17 p.m.

"Nelson and Parker should be here by now." I sit down on the couch and motion for Shay to join me. Her pacing is likely to give me a headache, and as my bruised and battered body does that quite well on its own, I'm relieved when she takes me up on my offer.

Across from us is Looney, a stand-alone chair that Mom's guests seldom sit on. Its patterns are so vibrant that they draw you in immediately. Its material is so soft that you could touch it for hours, and yet most people recoil because it appears cold and coarse. It faces the kitchen at an angle away from the couch; thus, it's a tad isolated and requires visitors to decide whether it's art they should admire from afar or a functional piece of furniture.

"What do you call that thing again?" Shay asks.

"Looney."

"Why do you and Gwen call it that?"

"Look at it—there's no way you'll sit in a chair like that unless you're missing a few screws."

"What does it say about the woman who bought it?" She snickers.

"Exactly."

I look down at my phone again.

"A watched pot never boils." She nuzzles her face into my neck and immediately apologizes. "I'm sorry—does that hurt?"

"No, it feels amazing to be close to you. I want your face nuzzled into every part of me," I confess.

There's a loud knock at the door—the kind that *Law & Order* has taught me to expect from a police officer or perhaps the FBI. Shay and I jerk up at the same time.

"Stay there, I'll get it." She walks over to the door.

Rain is starting to come down now, yet despite the drops, Parker and Nelson jockey for a position from which to hug Shay first.

Nelson has a wide smirk. With the relief of a child reporting that his sibling's the one who stole a cookie from the cookie jar, he rats out Parker: "I wanted to stop and get you flowers but Parker didn't want to stop!"

I laugh. "That sounds exactly right." I ease myself off the couch like a bloated pregnant woman and give them both a kiss hello, warning them to be gentle beforehand.

Nelson stares at Looney for a moment and ultimately decides to sit on it. I resolutely believe that my psycho-analysis-happy mother purchased this piece of furniture solely out of a desire to witness people's reactions to it—and in her absence, I'm the stand-in judge. Nelson tries to move it a smidge so he can face us, but when the hardwood floor screeches in protest, he shifts himself into an unnatural pretzel-like position with the lofty goal of trying to maintain eye contact.

Parker sits on the love seat to our left.

"I'll get beverages," Shay calls out, and I follow her into the kitchen. She's clanking cabinet doors open and closed. "I'm looking for something non-alcoholic to offer them."

I open the refrigerator and pull out four water bottles. It's not the bottles that take me back—it's the counting to four that undoes me.

Since high school it's been the four of us: booth for four at the diner, table for four for dinner, four beds on our tour bus, four stylists to dress us for interviews, four phones for our managers to hold while we play sold-out shows, the callout to start a song: one, two, three, four. And then we went from four to three, then three to two, and now, here we are again, and the innocuous act of getting four waters nearly bring me to tears.

Shay notices. "You okay?" She puts her hand gently in between my shoulder blades.

"Yeah, it's just, the four of us again—it hasn't been like this for a while. It just got me for a moment."

We walk back into the living room and Shay doles out the beverages. Parker greedily downs the whole bottle in three quick swigs.

Shay's eyes harden as she stares out the bay window. I look to see what she sees.

A snake of black Town Cars appears in front of the house as if out of nowhere. The sky shifts to a deeper black and opens up.

If you've ever wondered what it would look like if the President of the United States of America visited your home, you might envision black SUVs, men in dark suits and earpieces scouting your lawn, and maybe a helicopter circling overhead. Such a scene is only slightly less dramatic than what it's like when Bill Sweeney arrives. Almost immediately, I hear a knock at the door.

I shiver at the prospect of seeing Sweeney, the CEO of our record label. He is, after all, the same executive who allowed Parker to launch his solo career, leaving the rest of us to fend for ourselves. Flashbacks to Shay's hiatus makes me squeeze her hand in mine. All I care about is getting my band back together, and—I heave a sigh—Bill Sweeney is either going to be a friend or foe in that endeavor, and I don't yet know how he will shake out.

The first words out of Bill's mouth are like bullets to my chest. "Well, if it isn't the fantastic four, back together again," he calls out from the doorway in his Southern drawl.

"You always told us 'fame is your fate,' " I say back to him.

"Always did love that sassy sense of humor, Taryn."

Nelson stands up to offer Bill his seat. I wait with bated breath to see if he'll take it. My mother is right about one thing: it's fun to see how people react to Looney.

It's Bill's zero-fucks-given attitude that I truly loathe. Here he is, a guest, with not a gift in sight. I'm not saying he needed to bring a bottle of wine or flowers or a fucking cheesecake, but would it have been the right thing to do, yes. There are still active countdown clocks online tracking whether I'll live or succumb to my bruises (which is frankly just stupid, but still), some corner of the internet that thinks my passing is inevitable, and for all he knows, it could be true. To say the situation is awkward would be an understatement—this is next-level uncomfortable. Bill mother-fucking Sweeney is standing in my mother's living room, wearing a ten-gallon hat and a Western bolo tie, looking like a 1980s oil tycoon, without even so much as a Yankee Candle in his hands.

Bill takes a seat alone on the love seat, Nelson resumes his place on Looney, and Parker squeezes in between Shay and me.

"Now, I'm not really one for small talk so I'll get right to it."

I immediately pounce. "Yes, I *am* feeling a little better. Healing slowly, but I'm confident I'll continue to recover."

Bill coughs. "Of course, Taryn. My apologies. Where are my manners?"

"Well, go ahead," I say, waving him on. "I know you aren't here to chitchat."

"Maybe we should all start over?"

I narrow my eyes at Bill. "Now that's a loaded statement."

"Taryn." Nelson shakes his head back and forth.

"Now," Bill laughs, "don't go and tell me ya don't want to hear what I have to say?"

I laugh too. "Go on, Bill."

He peers intently at me. "I think I might have a proposition for the band."

I wince and make eye contact with Nelson, then Shay, and finally Parker.

We were prepared for this moment. You might say we are well rehearsed.

Bill leans forward. "Four Chords Music is interested in starting a small imprint. We've been doing our due diligence, and do you know the name that keeps floating around our offices?"

Nelson cradles the side of his face with the palm of his hand.

Bill tilts his head.

I look at Parker and then at Shay.

"Maroon 5?" Parker jokes, so Shay joins him: "Foo Fighters?"

"Oh, oh, One Direction?" Parker suggests.

Nelson nods his head solemnly.

Maybe it has something to do with the shift in power. A sense of agency overwhelms me. "Is it Pause For Effect, Bill?"

He stands up and walks around the living room, admiring every piece of furniture and photo that the room has to offer. "Your father," he says, shaking his head. "Such a shame."

Things already went south once with Bill Sweeney, and I will never let that happen again. It's going to take a lot more than a mention of my father to soften me up.

Nelson, who's still mostly oriented toward the kitchen, leans over, struggling to face Bill as he paces.

I close my eyes and move my head side to side. "What's made us deserving of your presence today, Bill?"

Bill is impossibly casual. He touches his hand to Nelson's shoulder and continues to walk past him. "The label and I have been thinking that Pause For Effect should get back together and release a new album on the imprint." He hovers above us, not stopping to take a breath: "Time is of the essence. We would need you to get back in the studio immediately so we can tie the album's release to the VMAs.

"The VMAs," Parker scoffs. "That's in August."

Bill sits back in his seat and looks only at Parker. "Of all of the group, I thought you'd be the one needing convincing. You sound like you're on board?"

Parker looks at Nelson, and then to me and Shay. "I am on board. It would be my pleasure to be back with them." He puts his hand on my leg.

"Ow," I grunt under my breath.

"Oh, so sorry." He immediately pulls away.

"Shay, you aren't saying much. How's all this sound to you, little miss?"

I am not sure that Bill ever intends to sound like a sexist Southerner, but I suppose intention doesn't matter when his words whittle her down to a grain of sand, to background noise. He leaves me no choice but to show him the women we have become.

I burst out in Shay's defense, "Bill, Shay and I are a couple, and there's no moving forward for us unless that's respected first and foremost."

Nelson backs me up. "It's true—we stand with Taryn and Shay."

Bill straightens out his bolo tie and the collar of his button-down.

"My apologies, I meant no disrespect." He laughs and his big belly bounces. "Now, that's all personal. Personal stuff. I want us to talk business."

"Oh, so like, 'don't ask, don't tell' for the music industry," Shay quips.

I shift my weight from one side to another. "This is a big proposal. Why aren't our lawyers a part of this conversation?"

Bill traces the arm of the love seat with his index finger. "I needed to smooth things over in person, no managers, no lawyers, just us."

"Maybe we just need some time alone, to digest this all," Nelson offers evenly, resetting the room to balance.

Bill slumps back.

"We have a few options, mate. We can break up, Parker can continue on with his solo career, or we can think about your offer."

"Fifteen million," Bill snaps impatiently.

"Fifteen fucking million what?" I squeal.

"Per band member?" Nelson claps back.

Bill turns to Parker. "Fifteen."

"Fifteen isn't shit to me," Parker says, "but I'd like my friends to be paid what they're worth." Bill shoots Parker a look sharp enough to slit his throat. His upper lip quivers. "Twenty million each for the next album," he says through gritted teeth.

Shay finally speaks up. "No thank you."

"Shay!" I yell. Then in a whisper: "Twenty million each," as if Bill isn't sitting a few feet from me.

"This whole thing reeks, Bill," Shay goes on.

"How so?" he asks in a tight voice.

"There's never any loyalty. Parker released his solo album with you and it killed our spirit, nearly killed our band, and you didn't care. You never explicitly said Taryn and I should keep our relationship under wraps, but it was implied. Then you schedule this impromptu meeting with us, not to see if Taryn's okay—she was an afterthought, if a thought at all. No, you're here without lawyers, without managers, because you're going to take advantage of us yet again. So I'm tapping out."

My mind rushes with the sounds of cash registers, visions of throwing out dollar bills like they do in money memes, and I want so badly to yell, "Twenty million! Shut up, Shay!" But I can't. Even though the last thing I want to do is jeopardize my band, with my heart so recently mended, I need to stand in solidarity with my love. I tell Bill, "If Shay's out, I'm out too."

Bill glances at Nelson, and he nods in the affirmative.

Parker crosses one leg over the other. He puts one hand on my leg (gently) and one on Shay's in solidarity and says, "I'm out too. I'm going to stick with the band this time."

"Well, if no means no then I ought to hit the road." Bill heads for the door and Nelson sees him out.

"I've never lost so much money so fast." I make a melodramatic crying face.

The snake of black cars disappears from the street almost as fast as it mysteriously appeared, slinking away slowly, the motor vehicle version of Bill Sweeney's walk of shame.

"Honey," Shay says, standing up with me and pulling me into a hug, "you're smarter than that."

"I'm not smarter than twenty million dollars, I'm not." I shake my head.

"But you are, honey." She brushes a wisp of hair out of my eye. "Bill just gave us the recipe to Coca-Cola. We just need to go recreate it."

I look at her quizzically when her other *other* half pipes up, "That's what I was thinking."

"Huh?" I shrug.

Nelson sits back down and finishes Shay's thought: "If Bill wants to do an imprint and he's low-key approaching Pause For Effect, it means whatever market research or insights they pulled, they gleaned that we're the way to monetize his big idea. So now all we have to do is start our own record label and release our own stuff.

"Is that all we have to do." I nod and laugh at Nelson's preposterous statement.

"That, and we *all* have to leave Four Chords." Shay sighs.

"It's that easy and that hard." Parker smiles.

"So are we doing this?" I ask no one and all of them at once.

"Fuck yes, we're doing this!" Nelson smiles.

Nelson claps Parker with one of those stupid man-to-man back-patting hugs.

Unlike Nelson and Parker who are too afraid to get intimately close, Shay and I embrace for a kiss. I pull in close to her and close my eyes, the sounds of jubilation from Nelson and Parker quiet down, but the raining money memes don't stop playing in my mind.

Through the living room window, the contours of the trees are hard to make out. Rain pummels the front steps in a drumroll-like symphony. Thunder claps loudly and the house sways. A strong wind whips and the lights go out.

The timing of the electrical outing is theatrical, perfectly spot-on. It's as if the house is acknowledging the symbolism and providing us with literal darkness to match the metaphorical darkness of the untimely death of our relationship with Four Chords. Even the house is saying, *It's over*.

The silence makes the beating rhythm of my heart sound louder. I squint to orient myself within the shadows. And then, as if by magic, the flow of electricity resumes, and the lights come back on.

Chapter 19
Memory Lane

The doorbell awakens me with a start. A melody playing on a loop, opaque lyrics trying to force their way from the back of my mind to the forefront. A dream in which the single best song ever written played out. At least that's how I felt about it as I was dreaming, and now that I've awoken, I can't recall a single syllable.

The doorbell rings again. "Okay, I'm coming, fuck," I yell out to no one in particular. I whisk myself downstairs and open the door.

"Hello, ma'am, my name is James, and I'm—"

I wave him off. "I'm sorry, James," I say with a yawn, "but I'm not really interested in buying any."

"Oh, no, ma'am," the young teenager laughs, "I was just saying that I'm from Forest Hills Florists and I have a delivery for you." He points down at the ground. There's a gigantic arrangement.

"What are these?" I lean over slowly to pick them up.

James dives down and brings them up to me. "Oh, these are an arrangement of Passion Flowers."

He shimmies out a card and begins to read it, "Thinking of you. Sending you love."

I snatch it from his hand. It's signed, Violette.

"Her timing is uncanny."

"I'm sorry, ma'am, what was that?"

"Oh nothing." I shake my head, "Hang on a second." Leaving the door slightly ajar, I go rummage through Mom's desk drawer. She must have money in here somewhere. But she doesn't.

I come back to the door. "I'm so sorry, James. I thought I had cash here, but I don't."

He smiles a big toothy grin. "It's okay, ma'am. Have a nice day."

I don't bother unwrapping the flowers. I just toss them on the floor near the garbage in the kitchen.

• • •

I run my fingers through my hair and hesitatingly place my right hand on the fading purple bruises on my skin as I walk back upstairs. The usual dull pain behind my eyes is non-existent. When I get to the top of the landing I smile when I realize, *I'm healing fast*. I take the painkillers off my end table and throw them into the trash. I think the rest of my recovery should happen *au naturel*.

A note, beautifully folded and carefully placed on the freshly made bed across from mine catches my attention. I shuffle my way over to pick it up:

Good morning, my sweetheart,
You were sleeping so peacefully that I couldn't bring myself to wake you. I ran out to get us coffee and will be back shortly.
I love you as much as I ever have.
Shay

"It's all-encompassing how much I love this woman," I mutter to myself. I kiss the paper and place it back down on the bed. At first, it doesn't seem like a good idea to start straightening up the room, but tidying is a habit deeply ingrained in me. It started when I was in middle school, in this very room. If things were messy, Mom would pop her head in and tell me, "a messy bedroom is a sign of a scattered brain."

I tackle something that doesn't require much energy: my desk. A small plastic bag of weed and rolling papers have fallen out of my bag. For a fleeting moment, I consider rolling a joint and sparking it up out the window to relive the true high school experience, but unlike my high school self, I actually concern myself with not embarrassing Mom. My hand brushes against my father's journal when I shove the weed and papers back in. I pull the journal out. While I have its color and shape memorized after carrying it around for years, I have, on many occasions, avoided holding it like this. I cradle it in my arms, stroke the cracked and worn leather binding with my thumb.

It's time to open it, pore over the lyrics scribbled in its liners, face the music so to speak.

In my father's handwriting, a line that sticks out like a misplaced tile in a mosaic: *For Taryn and Gwen*. My heart pumps fast as I stare at the words and think, *he wrote this*. It's unique to him. His handwriting lives on, here on this page. And yet, it's ephemeral. It will never be again. He will never write another letter, another syllable, another song.

There are scribbles upon scribbles of random lines etched across the pages till around halfway into the book. Some I recognize as lyrics of his songs; others sound like strings of poetry. There are some doodles of random objects in the corners. I flip through page after page after page until a blank page stares at me, the color yellowed with age.

I fish around in my bag for a pen, raise it to the page. I try to recall the song from my dream. I knew I should have written it down the moment I woke up, but I couldn't. The pen hangs there for a minute as the words slowly start to come back to me. I write, scratching out words and adding new ones as I go. The verses are there but the chorus eludes me.

"Ugh," I yelp, frustrated, and toss the old book toward my open closet. It just grazes my father's trunk and lands to the left of it. Staring me down from the corner of the closet is that big ol' trunk from World War II with its leather handles and rusted latches and cedar lining. It has made its way from my father's father, to my father, to me.

I grab a pillow off the bed and throw it down. Bracing myself, I gingerly kneel down in front of it. I open the lid and gaze down at the remnants of the past. Then I start to unpack every little piece of my father's puzzle. When I was younger, organizing his trunk helped me to feel closer to him. It's a collection of mementos: a dead Cartier watch, an old driver's license, a bow tie, a set of strings, piles of journals that house meandering letters about the mediocrity of the music industry. His writing vacillates between deep self-awareness and dangerous self-loathing.

It's challenging to find the right containers—both emotional and physical ones—to house the remnants of his past. *Compartmentalizing* is not just a phrase that my shrink mom throws around. I've never been able to fully survey the contents of the trunk. Usually, a few minutes in, I'll see something too depressing, read something too real, and slam the top closed. But today feels like it could be different.

I lift up a small box and a few pictures fall out of it. I've seen most of them before—my parents on their wedding day, Timothy Taylor and the Standards playing onstage, my father holding a hot dog at a BBQ. The photo captures him mid-laugh. I don't remember his laugh. How I long to hear what it sounds like.

With a gasp, I pick up an old guitar pick that's fallen to the floor. It's worn. I run it through my fingers. What show did he use it at? I pluck it with my thumb and toss it onto my desk. I'll take it with me when I leave. One of the few memories I have with my father is resting my head on his leg while he softly plucks his guitar, humming away to a song that floats in the air.

I thought my love of music really flourished within me when I first started to jam with Nelson and Shay. Parker will say it began when I met him. But my mother will insist until her dying breath that it was my father's influence that made me love music. It might be in my blood; it might be destiny. It's not like I will ever know for sure.

I don't know what I am looking for, but I keep searching anyway. I shift in my spot in front of the trunk, wavering between feeling overwhelmed and wanting to forge ahead to look for a mystery prize that I don't yet know exists. Surrounded by symbols of my father's broken past, a guttural moan escapes my mouth, and tears spring from my eyes. My eyes flicker to the mirror on the closet door, and I see the emotion sweeping through my face. The fading bruises stand out a little more on my face as the tears fall.

My feelings are confusing at best. How dare I cry over this man when I'm so mad that he's no longer here? And this paradox interlaced with my intermittent attempts to ravage my father's psyche, to learn who he was through what little he left me in the form of physical stuff. I sit there by the trunk, staring at a face in the mirror that his DNA created. I hunch over, put my head in my hands, and sob.

From my vantage point on the floor, I can see a mountain of clouds thunderously approaching. A tree with barren branches rubs against my bedroom window.

"You're up?" Shay startles me, walking into my room quietly. I lift my face from my hands and wipe away the tears to look up at her. She's holding two coffees. "Oh honey, what's wrong?"

I smile sheepishly, like a child who's done something she shouldn't have. "I'm okay. I was just going through some of *his* stuff."

I motion for her to come join me on the floor. She hands me a coffee and keeps one for herself.

"Well, it makes you uneasy, and that's normal, sweetie." She brushes away my tears from my cheek with her thumb.

"You could have made coffee downstairs." I take the paper cup with its flimsy plastic lid and take a sip.

"There's no place in the world like Queens for good diner coffee." She takes the lid off and blows on the surface to cool the temperature.

I take a sip.

We sit side by side among old papers, photos, and miscellaneous guitar strings. She has no idea what a valuable treasure trove she's next to; she's practically inside a rock and roll museum.

"Well, Shay, I'd like you to meet my father, Timothy." I wave my hand over the mess like Vanna White revealing a letter.

Shay raises her eyebrow, looking at the stuff around her. "Hello, Timothy," she says. Her eyes follow the line of fading bruises on my face. "Is it a coincidence that you're visiting your father this way after we agreed to get the band back together?" She cocks her head to one side playfully.

I laugh, though internally I'm stricken. "I hadn't even made that connection." I smile a bit. "Have you been talking to my mother?"

She shifts her weight to one side and crosses one leg over the other. "I haven't." She grins. "But I have one more observation for you."

"That is?"

"Maybe you're asking him for permission to follow in his footsteps."

I laugh. "I can't believe you think I need his permission."

She rolls her eyes. "Want. Not need."

Shay picks up my father's journal. "Haven't seen this since we were on tour." She holds it a little clumsily and the pages fan out. She apologetically folds it back together. "Here you go."

I steady my hand to receive it and we sit in silence.

"I've always been so curious about it . . ." Shay comments.

Looking down at the journal, I contemplate the gravity of this moment. I've spent most of my life concealing it, whisking it away—and here I am sharing her with him, and him with her.

Then I interrupt my own train of thought: "There's so much I need to say to you!" I yell it out so hard that I dizzy myself and rub my temples.

"Yeah." Shay shrugs. "About this weekend, I know, there's so much to unpack."

"No, no!" I furiously flip through the pages of the journal and get to where I started writing in the morning. I scrounge around, looking for a pen, and scribble on the page quickly.

Shay inclines her head toward me. "Are you finally going to share it with me?"

"Last night in my sleep, these words came to me, and when I woke up I knew I needed to write them down. But I just couldn't remember them."

She scoots over a little closer.

"You know," I muse, holding the journal a little out of reach, "I've never let someone in this close—" I point to the trunk. "To him."

"I know, and I'm touched."

"This is Timothy." I shuffle through the pages of the journal. "It's his thoughts, his doodles, his poetry."

She puts her coffee down and puts both hands up against her chest. "I'm honored that you're sharing this with me, Taryn."

I turn page after page until I land on where I was. "I started to build on one of his songs this morning. He had some words, and I added some as they came back to me, from my dream."

She looks down and reads it with a smile. "Not half bad for something you slapped together after you just woke up." She slowly runs her finger across the page and starts humming along a melody. Only every few words is audible.

I am elated, blood coursing through my veins. That it's Shay collaborating with me on some of my father's scribbles is exhilarating.

She races through it again, reading so fast, it sounds like she's reading the terms and conditions after a radio commercial.

She looks up at me and grins. "This is good." She motions. "May I use that pen?"

I offer it to her, and just as she's about to put it to paper she stops. "May I?"

"You may." I nod. She starts drawing arrows and scratching out words. It looks like she's scribbling out a football playbook.

"We move this to the chorus." She clears his throat. "Let's try it like this:"

"*You got what you wanted from me,*" Shay sings.

"*And I got what I needed,*" I join in.

"*You never let me speak my truth,*" she rejoins.

"*And now we're both in pieces,*" I whisper.

"*There's so much I need to say to you,*" we sing out together, our voices complementing each other effortlessly.

"Taryn, I can feel it in my bones, this is going to be a hit."

"It's pretty good," I say, modest and measured, but in my heart, I'm marinating in excitement.

In Shay I have not only a lover, but also a sister, mother, father, best friend, and whatever else I might be needing at the moment. And in this moment, she's someone who reminds me to have faith in our band once again. Pause For Effect now has a reason to get back out there.

Chapter 20
Exile

Mr. Kelsey's 120-decibel house alarm is going off when I walk into the kitchen. Gwen and Mom are suspiciously unmoved by the loud and piercing siren, conspiratorially gossiping about the news Shay and I shared with them last night about the band getting back together.

"Obviously, history proves that Parker is a hard person to trust," Mom says to Gwen as if I hadn't just walked into the kitchen.

"It's like being in an abusive relationship, Mom. She just wants to believe he'll change."

I sit down at the center island next to Gwen and give her the *are you shitting me* look.

"You know we love you," Mom tells me from her position in front of the oven, "but we just don't want you to be surprised if Parker disappoints the group again."

"I guess we'll find out soon enough whether he's changed or he's just good ol' Parker." I pour myself a glass of orange juice from the pitcher that's on the counter. "Is no one concerned about the sound blaring from Mr. Kelsey's house?" I block my ears with my hands.

Mom holds up five fingers, counts them down to one, and the sound disappears.

"How did you . . . do that?" I ask Mom.

"He's rewiring the system. He's done it before. It may go off again before the end of the day. Now eat, eat." Mom points to the spread on the breakfast island: a plate of bacon, a small bowl of strawberries and blueberries, syrup and butter for pancakes, the French press for coffee.

"Before I do—" I hand her the watch. "Here, I found this in his trunk yesterday."

"Oh, Taryn." She clasps it close to her chest. "You don't know how often I've looked for this watch. I never even thought to look in the trunk."

"The battery is dead."

"Oh, it doesn't matter." She slides her wrist into it. "You have no idea what a sign this is." She wags her pointer finger up to the roof. "I know you're with us, Timothy, you sly one! And a watch! Letting us know you're watching down on us. Ha! What a good sign, Timothy."

I press my lips, barely controlling my impulse to say something sarcastic, but Mom's beaming so I bite my tongue. I grab a piece of bacon from the plate. "Are there pancakes?" I motion to the syrup.

"I can only cook so fast, Taryn." Mom turns back to the burner. She shakes her wrist and wiggles the watch down her arm.

My gaze immediately shifts to Gwen, whose eyes well up with tears. "I'm not being mushy about the watch," she says, pushing the bacon away from her. "I just have a serious aversion to meat."

Mom puts her hand on her forehead and looks up, as if she can see the contents of the entire kitchen through her mind's eye. "I have biscuits in the oven, and I'm making pancakes on the griddle."

Unlike Gwen, I chomp down on the bacon.

"Why'd Shay sneak out this morning like she was on a walk of shame?" Gwen asks.

"If you must know," I say through another bite, "her father is gifting her the Montauk house, and she's on her way out there."

"Wait . . . what?" Gwen's voice raises a few notches. "Isn't that house worth like millions of dollars?"

"Yup." I pop my "p" to punctuate the point.

"Why?"

"He's gotta go back to the UK. The firm's opening up another office there. He thinks he'll be there for a few years and so he's giving it to her."

"But just her? Why not her and Nelson?"

"Their father's buying a place in London and the deal is, in a few years he's gifting that to Nelson."

"How fucking loaded is he?"

"Beyond … like private jet loaded."

"So, are you guys, like, moving back in together?"

Mom stands a little taller when Gwen asks this, her back still turned to us.

"We talked about it last night and I think I want to live with her in Montauk, yes. We're on tour a lot, and we can come stay here and visit you and the baby, and you and Bradley can come out. It'll be amazing."

"Well, if it's so important, why aren't you with her now?"

"Um, I worry about you, Gwen."

"Why?"

"I don't know, because boundaries? When a parent gifts you a home, you don't bring your on-again-off-again girlfriend to the table. It's just not the time yet. It's not like we're married."

"Fuck, for that house *I'd* marry her."

"Lovely. Besides, I want to stay home today and finish the writing we were working on yesterday."

"So your merry little band of mock-stars is getting back together?"

I roll my eyes at her. "Shay and I wrote our first song together last night."

"Do you even write songs? Are you like a songwriter now?"

"Well, I don't, but now I guess I do. Kind of like how you weren't pregnant and then all of a sudden, *poof*, you were. It's the same journey."

"Hardly the same journey."

"Actually, you're right, my journey involved our father."

"You, Shay, and Dad—what a trifecta."

"Honey," interjects Mom, "what do you mean? How did your father help out?"

"I had this melody stuck in my head like an earworm, so I sat down to get it all out and Shay and I worked on a song together. His journal has all these scribbled notes and lines, and we used them for lyrics."

Mom stands still in wonderment. "That is just beautiful, Taryn. Absolutely beautiful." She rummages through the drawers. "Aha, I knew I had you here!" She holds up a sage smudge stick. "You light this and wave it over the old book. It'll cleanse it of any negative energy."

I take the bundle of sage and grin at Gwen. "Oh, okay, Mom, I will."

Gwen smirks at me. She looks down at her phone. "One hundred and fifty-four days," she sings out.

"I guess this is too much talk about me for more than sixty seconds." I shrug. "Enlighten us; what's happening in one hundred and fifty-four days?"

She waves her phone in the air. "This app is amazing. It tells you everything about pregnancy. It just sent me an alert about my due date."

"It's like a countdown clock?"

"Well, yes, I suppose."

"I wish I had a countdown clock app."

"For what?"

"Anything." I shrug. "I don't know, maybe how long until the next time Parker blows everything up."

Gwen laughs. "They definitely don't make an app for that."

"Technically, Taryn—" Mom removes her watch, flattens it out on the center island, and rolls up her sleeves. She puts on her mitts and pulls a tray of biscuits from the oven. "You and Parker are equally complicit in these years-long theatrics. You both have a lot of growing up to do."

I take a sip of juice. "Is that your professional opinion, doctor?"

She sets the sheet on the stove with a bang. "Just a mom-servation." The smell of biscuits wafts through the air.

I flip the watch over and see an inscription on the back. It's a date. "What's this date mean?"

"It's the date I met your father." She pulls the oven mitt off her hand like a doctor pulls off a rubber glove.

I turn the watch right-side up and squint, then nod and put it back down. Mom puts the watch back on her wrist and shakes it. The watch moves down her arm a bit.

"One would think you wouldn't need a watch to remember the date."

"Don't be so immature, Taryn." Gwen's tone is dripping with disdain.

"Immature? Jesus. You already sound like Mom. A mom. Our mom."

Mom walks across the room to open the window half an inch. "Just enough to bring in a taste of the winter air." I turn around and notice the flowers from Violette on the counter. "Mom, why did you put those out? I left them by the trash."

"Oh, honey, these are beautiful. Why would you throw these away?"

"They're from Violette." I grin.

"How did she even know you were staying here? How did she get Mom's address? That's borderline stalking!" Gwen yells out.

"I don't know." I shrug. "Her publicist, probably."

"It's not nice to discard living entities, but we shouldn't have that kind of energy in here, not with *Shay* around." Mom whispers Shay's name as she places a platter of biscuits in front of Gwen.

Gwen furiously types into her pregnancy app. "Are these cream biscuits? My app says I should avoid cream biscuits."

Mom shrugs. "In my day, we smoked when we were pregnant."

"Well, this isn't the early 1900s, Mom," Gwen shrieks.

"They're not cream and they're fine. Have one, honey, and relax. I'm more concerned about how much you worry than I am about biscuits." Mom smiles warmly.

I throw my head back and laugh—and then relief washes over me. The motion didn't cause the shocking pain I expected it to. Gwen is picking apart the biscuit.

"Oh, for fuck's sake, Gwen, just eat it." I snap.

Mom puts her hand over Gwen's so that Gwen puts her phone down and takes a bite of the biscuit.

"It's not easy, you know. Everything is off limits when you're pregnant," Gwen tells me sternly.

"I'm sorry."

"Do you have any idea how scared I am?" It's her tone more than her words which resonates with me. I hadn't thought about what it must be like to be Gwen right now.

Mom hands each of us a plate with three pancakes drizzled in syrup.

I turn to Gwen. "I'm used to you sabotaging relationships, and maybe I'm afraid you might sabotage this one too, with Bradley."

"What do you mean?" Gwen says, a little offended.

"You always picked the wrong guys and sabotaged yourself into heartbreak."

"You're right," Gwen says softly, looking down at her plate of pancakes. "But he's different."

I nod in agreement. "He's different." But what I don't dare ask is, *are you?*

Gwen pushes the plate of pancakes away from her. "It's the syrup smell." She scrunches her face.

"Well, I can get that out of the way for you." Mom shuffles the plates around and moves the food closer to the stove, away from Gwen.

I fall into the role of proxy caretaker for Bradley and rub Gwen's back. Then I fill the glass in front of her with orange juice.

A wry smile possesses my face. The realization that Gwen has something that I do not, that she accidentally stayed one step ahead of me—I'm feeling what can only be constituted as jealousy. It's a great epiphany for me to understand that she too seeks the love and adoration of a partner, perhaps even more than me. Though it might have seemed like I was going to be the first one to have a child, she beat me. She's going to be the first one to make our mother a grandmother.

So much of my praise has come in bigger packages—roaring crowds, sold-out shows, armies of fans, songs on the radio—but that's no more meaningful than becoming a mother. I've been so consumed with competing within my career that it's never occurred to me that Gwen is worth competing with too.

"What are you thinking? You look so lost in thought." Gwen takes a sip of orange juice.

I shake my head. "I just was thinking."

"About?"

"Oh, a line came to me. I think maybe I'll save it for a song."

"What's the line?"

"The birth of something new is also the death of something old."

She says it out loud a few times fast. "Yeah, cool, I like it."

Chapter 21
Luxury Problem

Summer is almost over. I know this because the days are getting shorter, the air less thick, and Gwen's due date imminent. Gwen's high blood pressure caused her ob-gyn to put her on bedrest. She is absolutely huge. Stunning and glowing, but huge. She and Bradley are staying at Mom's for the final stretch of her bed-ridden pregnancy. He's already taken leave from racing for a bit.

I moved out of Mom's and in with Shay three months ago. Having a house on the beach during the summer has conjured up all types of inspiration. We've even discussed holding our wedding there. I don't know which is more incredible—that I get to wake up every day to the sound of waves crashing against the beach, or Shay.

These days, Mom doesn't have to cry much about an empty nest. With Gwen and Bradley planning to stay there for a while with the baby, the pendulum has swung all the way back to full house.

There was definitely something about staying at Mom's after my breakup and through my recovery that helped me to heal quickly, or at least I felt like it helped. Whatever the reason, I'm back and better than ever.

• • •

Even though it feels like years have elapsed, it's only been five months since Nelson, Shay, Parker, and I terminated our contract with Four Chords Music and announced that Pause For Effect are officially back together. In perfect time too. The Video Music Awards arrive like clockwork at the end of every summer, and this year we're nominated in a new category: *Trailblazers*.

We haven't dropped our album yet, so our new publicist, Bonnie, told us that she thinks the new category was created just for us. She also heard a rumor that Bill Sweeney tried to fight our nomination. Fuck that guy.

We're running late to the VMAs, so late in fact that when our limo pulls up to the red carpet, Pause For Effect and Bonnie all but fall out of it. As we walk the red carpet, Parker blows kisses at the paparazzi and Nelson bestows the onlookers with the Queen's wave. Bonnie leans in close on my right-hand side, whisper-talking in my ear, giving us the rundown of who everyone is as we pass:

"Second camera on your right is E!"

Bonnie subtly darts in front of me, blocking Vulture from getting a shot of me from what she dubs "not your best angle."

"Kara Longione from SLZ Media on your left," she murmurs.

Parker notices several cameras trained on him; he breaks out his camera-ready smile.

Our stylists convinced Shay and I to wear white suits and white pumps. The heels give Shay a good few inches above me. In fact, we're all wearing white—an act of solidarity, a symbol of our projected innocence, the color of perfection. The suits are great and all, but they don't have pockets. We've handed our phones to Bonnie for safekeeping, and I feel a bit naked without mine.

Bonnie leans in. "*People* magazine is to our left, so let's please keep walking. Remember, this is *your* comeback." She waves her arms, motioning for us to head inside the theater.

Bonnie's got a bit of anxious energy about her, but if it keeps us on track, I guess I can tolerate it. In the limo ride over, she went on a tear about how this is a critical comeback moment for Pause For Effect. It's the first show we're playing together as a band since our breakup. When she noticed our attention waning, she turned to Nelson and likened our comeback to the royal family. This caused him to sit up straight and pay attention.

"Everyone tunes in to watch the royal wedding. Even if they hate weddings, even if they hate the Brits. For one day, everyone in America is an Anglophile. Know why?" she asked us like a schoolteacher addressing a group of kindergarteners.

"Because it's all about the tension. The reveal. The mystery of it all. You only have one opportunity to bask in the comeback moment. After tonight, it's over, you've come back. From tomorrow on, you're only as good as the last great thing you did, and the last great thing you did better be winning tonight."

· · ·

The VIP bar is packed, and I try not to gawk every time I see a celebrity. Even though I know I'm a celebrity too. I stare at the ornate railings on the staircase, the chipped gold-encrusted carvings, the hand-painted mural behind the balcony, but I stay right here, grounded on this level.

Shay grabs my hand and stops me. Nelson, Parker, and Bonnie keep walking, not realizing that Shay's pulled me into a corner. The noises of the crowd fade away as the people clear out of the bar and go back to their seats.

"Shay—" I push a stray piece of hair behind her ear. "What are you doing?"

"I just need a minute of your time," she says, putting her hands around mine and kissing them.

I breathe softly as she looks at me with her bedroom eyes. "You can have all the minutes of my time," I tell her.

She laughs. "That's what I'm going for."

"What do you mean?"

"Taryn, I love you. I've loved you for years without ever faltering. Even when we were apart, the only constant in my life was my love for you. It's always been you." Her fingers gently brush the side of my face.

"I love you too, Shay," I whisper, "more than yesterday, but less than tomorrow."

She smiles. "I'm glad to hear you say that because . . ." She pauses as she lets go of my face and reaches into her pocket to pull out a small box. I gasp audibly when I see the box, gasp again when she pulls out the ring.

"Shay . . ." I squeal as tears start to form in the corners of my eyes.

A platinum band with diamonds dancing around its circumference. It's perfect. She takes my hand into her shaky hand, doesn't even have the chance to get the words out. I beam. "Yes, yes, of course! Yes!"

She places the ring on my finger, then pulls me in for a kiss. My hands clutch her waist and my face presses against hers. I can taste the salt of her tears, or maybe they're mine? We break apart and laugh excitedly. I'm feeling slightly dazed, as if I'm outside of my body, watching myself experience this moment.

"Congratulations!" Nelson's voice startles me and forces my attention back into focus. He envelops us in a bear hug. I whip around to see Parker grinning from ear to ear and invite him in for the embrace too.

"I call dibs on best man," Parker jokes.

Shay smooths out her brother's collar. "I guess that leaves you as the maid of honor."

"Ha, ha." Nelson smirks.

Bonnie bursts through the doors. "You've got to get to your seats. They're about to announce the nominees, and Pause For Effect needs to be sitting together for the reaction shot. The camera is going to pan to you four!"

I nod at Bonnie and we follow her as she charges through the doors of the theater and gets us to our seats.

I don't even hear Pause For Effect being announced—I just know that one minute we're seated, and the next, we're being whisked onstage. At home, Mom, Gwen, and Bradley are watching, probably glued to their social networks to see how our fans dissect every syllable of our thank you speech. A speech personally crafted by us, much to Bonnie's dismay. In her words, "Your ninety-second thank you speech can make or break your comeback almost as much as the award itself."

The lights are bright and cause pinpricks of sweat to form on my neck.

Nelson is wearing a face that reads, *I'm still shocked that our name was called.*

Parker looks as comfortable here in the middle of our group as he does on any stage.

And Shay—I've never seen Shay beam like this.

We've practiced this, we're well-rehearsed, and while the crowd might expect Parker to wander onto the stage looking scattered and uttering four-letter words, he begins:

"The last year of our lives has held some of the hardest, most amazing, and bizarre times."

He steps to the side and I move to the center: "Many of those times have been public, and some not-so-public."

I shimmy to the side and Nelson dips his head down to the mic: "We want to thank our fans for being Pause For Effect's constant."

Nelson pulls Shay in and they share the podium together. "It's been a lot of good," Shay says. She scooches back and I lean my head in. "We're lucky to be here and we know it."

We yell in unison, "Thank you so much. We love you!"

• • •

When we get offstage, Bonnie greets us. "Congratulations!" She envelops us in a hug but pulls back quickly. "Sorry to break up the moment, but Taryn, I think you need to check your phone." She hands it over. There are seventeen messages and thirteen missed calls from my mother, Bradley, and Gwen.

"Holy shit!" I exclaim as I look through my phone.

"What's wrong?" Shay asks.

"We have to leave."

"Leave? What about the after-party?"

"I know," I say, turning her with wide eyes, "but Gwen's water just broke."

Chapter 22
Tell Me with Your Eyes

"There was traffic," I announce as we walk into the room. As if our arrival status is as momentous as Gwen having a baby.

You'd think that on the way to the hospital, I would have ruminated on how grateful I am that she and Bradley are going to make me an aunt, but I didn't. All I could think was, oh my fucking stars, Gwen is about to become a mom.

Nothing is happening. It's not the scene I thought we would walk into. But I guess my only point of reference for what happens during childbirth is what I've seen on TV.

Gwen is sitting up slightly in her hospital bed, looking, dare I say it, as normal as ever. No sweaty forehead, no screaming—she's just chilling out, watching a video on her phone. And Bradley's another poster child for calm and collected. Just sitting on the bed opposite her, looking up at the TV, holding the remote in his left hand.

Shay and I hug him first and then make our way over to Gwen, who exclaims, "I am so glad you're here."

"Are you kidding me?" I reply. "I wouldn't miss this for the world."

"Congrats on the win, *Trailblazers!*" Bradley grins a toothy grin. Shay and I laugh.

"You can now insist people call you 'award-winning.' " Gwen shifts and screws up her face in a pained look. "What's on your finger?"

"Yeah," I wave my ring finger around, "so this happened."

Gwen tries to sit up straighter but abandons the attempt. "I am way more excited than my movement allows for." She holds her arms up and I climb into her embrace.

Shay leans down to hug Gwen. The door to the bathroom opens and Mom pops out of it. "The gang's all here," she says.

"Well, most of us. Nelson and Parker had to stay." I kiss Mom hello.

"Show her the ring," Gwen yells out.

I wave my hand in front of Mom. "Shay's going to make an honest woman out of me."

Mom hugs Shay and me simultaneously. "What an exciting night! How was the show? We were watching it."

"The show was awesome," I tell her.

Mom sings out, "That's because it's a new moon. It's a great time for new beginnings." She nods to Bradley and Gwen. "For both of you as well." As Mom walks past

Bradley on the spare bed, he bolts up and motions for her to sit. They compromise and sit together on it.

"I cannot believe you guys are going to be parents," I say, vacillating between relief that my sister is first to become a mom and alarm that it's really happening.

Gwen smiles and opens her mouth to say something, then stops mid-breath and clutches the sheets. "Just— one—minute." Her face wrinkles and her body gets tight. I look at Shay and then at Bradley and then at Mom. Gwen stays like that with her face scrunched in pain and then returns to the conversation. "Sorry, that one was a little rough."

"Was that a contraction?" I ask, almost shouting.

"No, it was an orgasm," Gwen says languidly.

"You joke, but I'm pretty sure an orgasm is what got you here."

"The doctor told me this could go on for hours."

"Hours?" I spit back. "No one's checked on you since we got here."

Gwen puts her phone in front of her face and resumes watching the video she was poring over when we walked in. It's one of her own makeup tutorials. She's critiquing it frame by frame.

Bradley stands up, so Mom lies down across the spare bed. He paces the room until Gwen pulls his sleeve and asks him to "please stop."

Finally, a nurse arrives. She rolls in a "father cot" for Bradley, and I note the sexism inherent in even the name of an extra piece of furniture. Bradley switches the TV on and flips through channels in a rapid succession. His anxious energy isn't lost on any of us, but Gwen finds it most grating. "Please, sweetie, settle on one channel."

"The nurse doesn't even stay in here?" I object, slightly horrified at what little supervision this whole ordeal commands.

"She comes in to check my vitals." Gwen, doesn't even look up from her phone as she responds to me.

Bradley lands on the channel playing reruns of the '90s sitcom *Seinfeld*. "I'm a sucker for this show," he says, settling back into the *father cot*.

First, we watch the episode about the puffy shirt.

"This one's classic," Bradley tells us. "Jerry accidentally agrees to wear a pirate shirt on *The Today Show*." He laughs to himself.

And then the episode where they go to the Hamptons, and Bradley indulges us with the plot: "George has shrinkage from being in the pool."

I think to myself, Montauk, the Hamptons. I live there now.

I look at Gwen to see if she's noticed that at the cusp of her giving birth, her famous motocross-loving boyfriend has suddenly, near-instantly transformed to a dad—right down to clutching the remote as he laughs out loud to outdated sitcoms.

She hasn't noticed. She's in between contractions, drifting in and out of pain.

When the next episode comes on, Bradley regales us with his superior sitcom knowledge. "This is a landmark episode. It's about masturbation. They have a contest of who can go the longest without doing themselves."

I don't have the heart to tell him he's probably going to embark on his own masturbation contest once my sister gives birth.

The entire Gwen-going-into-labor ordeal has waned from "Holy fucking shit I'm going to be an aunt" to a degree of mundanity only matched by waiting in line at the DMV.

Shay hangs her head low. I can tell she's tired. We all are. It's been a tremendous day, filled with tears of joy and fear from every side of the spectrum. She looks up at me and smiles. Despite the fluorescent glow from the television against her face, it's a perfect smile. The kind of smile I can get lost in. The kind of smile attached to the kind of woman I can marry. The kind of woman I will marry.

Parker texts, *Has Gwen pushed out a human?*

I hold my phone up and show it to Gwen. "He makes everything sound more dramatic than it needs to be."

"I know." She nods. Then she gets another contraction.

"Gwen. You should rest for now. We should go."

She nods tiredly.

"I'm really happy for you both." I smile gratefully at my sister and watch as Bradley softly combs his fingers through her hair. Then I put my arm out for Shay to grab. "C'mon, we should go home for a little while."

I lean over to kiss Gwen on the forehead. She opens her eyes drowsily and I tell her, "Shay and I are going to go to Mom's to get some sleep. We're fifteen minutes away if anything changes here."

• • •

A few hours later, Mom's threatening text wakes me up. *Get here now! The contractions are four minutes apart! She's seven centimeters dilated.*

Shay grabs her camera bag and we run out the door.

Shay is weaving in and out of traffic when Mom texts, *The doctor told her to start pushing.*

We probably would've made it up just in time if the elevator didn't take seven minutes to appear. As we wait, I anxiously push the button and think about my short-term stint as a smoker in high school. I'd time how fast I could smoke a cigarette. The four-minute break between classes was thirty seconds more than I needed to have a smoke. As we get in to the elevator, I say to Shay, "If I smoked, I could've finished two cigarettes by now." She shrugs, assuming I'm just guessing. But I know that the time we waited was exactly as long as I needed to have two cigarettes.

It was also exactly how much time Gwen needed to give birth.

"It's a girl," Mom announces proudly when we walk through the door.

"Her gender isn't what's most important, Mom." I beam as I make my way over to Gwen, who steadies her newborn against her chest. "She's a perfect little human," I shout-whisper when I finally see her.

I bend down to look at my niece. Not look, stare. I stare at her in a way that would make most adults uncomfortable. Her soft skin and chubby cheeks are delicious.

I'm waiting for my father. I don't realize it at first, but I am. Not for him to physically walk in—I know that won't happen. I'm simply waiting for someone to mention him, share a memory, wish that he could be here to share this moment.

I look back down at the baby. She has our father's eyes. I purse my lips and think to myself, *Hmm, look at that, he is here after all, housed inside the cells of this beautiful little person.*

"You must be a proud papa," Shay says to Bradley as she kisses him hello. "Congratulations to you both." She places her camera down on the end table.

I spend the better part of the next several hours texting and sending photographs to everyone I know, including Nelson and Parker. *Where the fuck are you two? They're going to release her from the hospital before you even show up.*

We're on our way, Parker shoots back almost instantaneously.

The upside of them not showing up immediately is that Gwen is able to catch a nap. Or at least something loosely resembling a nap. The baby mostly sleeps while Gwen does. She fusses from time to time, and when she does, Gwen feeds her, and then they close their eyes again. Mom can't stop telling us what a good baby she is, as if any one of the four of us know what a good baby behaves like.

Gwen shifts and opens her eyes, staring directly at me as if she's just asked me a question and is waiting patiently for me to answer.

"What do you need?" I ask her.

"Some water," she responds in an exhausted whisper.

I walk outside the room and look for a drinking fountain. The look of confusion on my face causes a nurse wearing neon pink scrubs with bright blue bunny rabbits to ask, "Water station?"

"Yes."

She points in an easterly direction. "Over there."

Walking back to the room with a full pitcher of water, I see Nelson and Parker hovering outside the door to Gwen's room.

"Look who I found," I announce.

"Come in, come in." Mom waves to Nelson and Parker.

Nelson makes a beeline for Gwen. "A girl?" he says. "Does Taylor DNA even make boys?"

"Not now," Mom hisses. "Taryn doesn't want you whittling her niece down to a gender."

I snap my head around. "It's true, I don't."

Nelson whips out his phone. "May I?"

"Yes, just don't get me in it." Gwen lifts her head up.

Shay hovers on the other side of Gwen's bed, across from Nelson. "You've never looked so beautiful, Gwen."

"I've never felt so beautiful and looked so shitty," Gwen responds.

Nelson walks over and hugs Bradley. "I reckon this is the best day of your life."

"Just about, yeah." Bradley smiles.

"I have a granddaughter," Mom says to Parker.

"You do, Marge. You have a beautiful granddaughter." Parker hugs Mom, and then he walks past her to the other mom, the new one, Gwen. "Does she have a name?" he asks as he leans down to admire the newest member of the family.

"Gwen's working on a name," Mom responds.

Mom doesn't walk—she doesn't even saunter—she *glides* across the room as if her elation in becoming a grandmother makes her body defy gravity, makes her move without touching the floor.

Gwen acknowledges what she's been avoiding: the insurmountable task of naming the baby. She admits that she's not afraid to raise or nurture a child. She's prepared to start teaching her all she needs to know about the world. But the task of giving her a name—that's much more of a challenge than she realized.

"You must have discussed a name. You've had over nine months." I look to Gwen and then to Bradley.

Bradley opens his mouth, pauses, and then starts, "I want to honor my mom somehow. I just haven't been able to come up with a good way to do it."

When Bradley mentions his mother, the room becomes quieter. The energy feels apprehensive.

"We were thinking of naming her Kimbra, a name that combines *Kim*, his mother, and *Bradley*," Gwen says. She takes a sip of her water.

Kimbra? Kimbra sounds like the name of a fucking Pokémon character, I want to yell at her. But I can't tell her the name she's considering, with the word "bra" falling off the end of it, is ripe ground for bullying by schoolkids. In life, sometimes, you have to bite your tongue. You have to repress the joke. You have to act like a mature adult and accept that maybe it's the discomfort about Kim's death that compels me to want to make the joke in the first place. Maybe an homage to her, in whatever form, is beautiful. They want Kim's legacy to live on, which seems like a lot of pressure for a seven-pound eight-ounce brand-new human, but I know my niece can handle it. She's a Taylor, after all.

"Kimbra is a beautiful name." I yawn and then immediately apologize for it. "Wait, is she a Taylor or a Collins?"

"Oh, the theatrics," Parker chides. "What is this child's family name?"

"Well, Bradley and I aren't married," Gwen admits as if we were concerned that we had missed their wedding.

Gwen's phone is ablaze with buzzers, dings, and vibrations at a steady pace of one every thirty seconds.

"Well, is she a Taylor or a Collins?" Mom asks, suddenly in the conversation.

I raise my hand to my face and grab my bottom lip, waiting patiently.

"Kimbra Collins," Bradley pipes in and then looks at Gwen. She nods affirmatively.

Shay picks up her camera and looks at Gwen with a *May I?* look on her face.

Gwen heaves a deep sigh. "But I don't have any makeup on."

Shay crouches down beside her bed so that she's at eye level with the baby and looks up at Gwen. "In twenty years, you won't care about the makeup. You'll care about reliving the moment." Shay grabs Gwen's hand and holds it. "Give me smeyes."

"Smeyes?" Gwen asks through wet eyes.

"Just smile with your eyes."

Gwen dabs underneath each eye to blot the tears. "Okay, fine," she says, her voice cracking. She wears an apologetic smile across her worried face.

Shay repositions her slightly. Gwen rolls her shoulders back and looks down at her baby, then up at Shay and gives her smeyes.

• • •

I wave at Mr. Kelsey when we pull up at Mom's. He's kneeling down on his front pathway, removing the weeds growing between the paving stones with what looks to be a butter knife. I point at the two-tone minivan in Mom's driveway and laugh with Shay. "See, I told you he really bought one!"

"You weren't kidding, huh."

"Nope, he got it before she even gave birth."

"He's a nice guy. I like him." Shay pulls into the driveway, just behind the two-tone minivan that Bradley bought.

• • •

Mom warns us as she opens the door, "She wears Kimbra every moment she gets, like the baby's a statement piece she bought at Barneys."

Gwen's sitting on the couch. She sports gray half-circles under her eyes. She hasn't worn this little makeup since Mom gave birth to her. She and Bradley are showered, though, and despite their general tired demeanor, they look pretty well put together.

"Aren't new parents supposed to look disheveled?" Shay drops her bag down on Looney. "You both look great."

"Mom watched the baby so we could shower." Gwen peeks down at her chest and smiles at Kimbra, who is fast asleep.

"Yeah, Marge has been amazing," Bradley says. "I don't know what we would do without her."

Shay smiles at Mom, and Mom straightens an invisible crown on her head.

Gwen's clothes are scattered about everywhere. "Mom isn't your maid."

"Why can't you shut up?" she barks. "Sorry, I didn't mean to yell."

"Jesus, that was an inappropriate reaction."

"I know. My hormones are all over the place."

Shay turns to Bradley. "Is the baby sleeping through the night?"

"*He's* sleeping through the night," Gwen says, pointing at Bradley, "But I'm breastfeeding so Kimbra and I are up every three hours."

"Every three hours," I repeat. "Is that typical?" I open my eyes wide at Shay.

"Oh stop it." Shay waves me off. "If you can pull all-nighters to play shows, you can wake up every three hours for a baby."

"Wait," Gwen gasps. "Are you pregnant?" She tilts her head in disbelief.

"No!" Shay and I say at the same time. "Just talking about it." I add.

Kimbra moves a bit and tries to settle into a comfortable spot.

I yelp. "Those cheeks!"

Kimbra slowly opens her eyes and I hold my arms out for her. Gwen peels Kimbra out of her carrier, revealing the shocking display of her cleavage. She hands her over to me and I lift my niece up to my shoulders, instinctively rocking her and patting her back simultaneously.

I crane my neck out slowly so I don't disturb Kimbra. "I cannot believe how huge your breasts are." I point at Gwen.

Self-consciously, she covers up.

"Does it—" I scan the breastfeeding machine and bottles surrounding it on the end table. "Does it hurt?"

"Well," she pauses, "it's not fucking fun." She stands up and walks around the living room, picking up baby accoutrements to shove into the diaper bag: diapers, wipes, a burp cloth.

"Dairy, gluten, and caffeine decrease your supply. So basically, I can't ingest anything fun if I want to breastfeed."

I look over at Bradley. He just shakes his head side to side. "I'm fine with formula. Lots of kids are raised on formula." He shrugs.

I look down at my niece and continue the bouncing and swaying motion.

Gwen slings the diaper bag over her shoulder and shoves a giant pair of Audrey Hepburn sunglasses onto her face. "C'mon, let's go."

"You haven't told me where we're going?" I follow her anyhow, keeping my pace steady so I don't wake up Kimbra, who is now fast asleep in my arms.

"Honey, you just gave birth three days ago. Are you sure you want to go out?" Mom asks in a concerned but loving tone.

"Mom, I need fresh air." Gwen shoves her keys into the front pocket of the diaper bag.

"Gwen, you've stayed indoors longer to binge-watch *Six Feet Under* in one sitting," I remind her.

"There's something we need to do." She smiles warmly at Bradley, and he tilts his head at her and smiles back. "C'mon. Let's go before I start bleeding through my mesh panties."

I peel Kimbra off me and pass her back to Gwen but I must have moved too swiftly and the baby wails. Gwen settles Kimbra by placing her on her chest.

"They are good boobs," Bradley says to his daughter. "They calm me down too." He kisses Kimbra on the back of her head.

Mom plops down on the couch and watches as we head toward the door. "Please be safe with my granddaughter."

Gwen turns around and shifts Kimbra into her wearable baby carrier. "Get up! You're coming too!"

"I am?"

"You are," Gwen sings.

Mom follows the steadfast directive and grabs her bag from the closet.

"Bradley!" Gwen is rummaging through the diaper bag with one hand. "Her binky. I think I left it upstairs," she demands.

"Her binky?" My eyes open wide and Shay's meet mine. I'm confident we are thinking the same thing: that Gwen is already using cutesy words for baby gear.

Bradley puts his arm on mine. "It's a pacifier."

He runs upstairs. He returns a little out of breath, holding an aqua blue pacifier.

"Got it."

• • •

The clouds barrel across the sky as we arrive at the Gates of Heaven cemetery.

A burial is taking place. The priest is the spitting image of Ted Bundy. His presence at the freshly dug grave is distressing, to say the least. With his thick eyebrows and healthy physique, he has to know that his physical resemblance to one of the country's most notorious killers is unfortunate.

We all look straight ahead, careful not stare too long at the burial. Bradley places the diaper bag on the bottom of Kimbra's stroller. We walk quite a distance along the winding cemetery road, stopping twice so Bradley can fuss with the stroller and make sure that the bag is still in place.

The grass is still wet from the rain earlier, and the thick green blades stick to our shoes. Our father's plot is the shape of a Sicilian pizza slice, adorned by a black marble slab. Gwen stands stiff and then bends down to fiddle with the wilting daisies in front of his headstone; nearly dead flowers for a totally dead father. I scan the other headstones. They all have wilting daisies. I guess the groundskeeper leaves them.

Shay and I sit on the wet grass and immediately regret it, so we shimmy over to the pavement just off to the side of his headstone. Gwen smirks at me, and I reply with a sullen nod. I know she's suppressing an uncomfortable laugh. She puts her hand on my shoulder—she's beginning to squat down beside me on the ground, but the uncomfortableness of this motion is apparent on her face. Bradley jumps up to help her and Mom instinctively grabs the stroller from him.

Gwen waits a beat and then begins to tell a story to our father's grave: "Labor started while Bradley and I were eating Chinese takeout, but I thought it was coming all day. My stomach was itching when the contractions started. During the hospital tour, they'd warned us about Braxton-Hicks, so I ignored the sensations and figured the baby would never come this early. But the contractions came closer and harder, so much so, I couldn't focus on the fried rice I was looking forward to devouring. The contractions went from every hour to every thirty minutes, and by the time Bradley offered me my fortune cookie, I told him he was going to have to get me to the hospital."

There isn't a dry eye here. Except for Kimbra's because she's still fast asleep.

"Tim, Bradley's such an impressive father already. You would be so proud." Mom gets the words out through her quivering lips.

I sniffle and take my turn. "Gwen had the audacity to have the baby the night my band won an award." I laugh as tears roll down my face.

Shay squeezes my hand. "Timothy, your granddaughter is so beyond lucky to be loved by this family."

Bradley procures a tissue from his pocket and laughs as he blows his nose. He pulls his black satin necklace out from under his shirt and gives it a kiss. "Mom, Gwen gave birth to a perfect, healthy, beautiful little girl, and the least we could do was name her after you." Bradley croaks out a high-pitch sob. He's speaking directly to the necklace balled up in his hand, his mom's ashes in the vessel.

"Mom," Gwen says, "would it be okay—" She stops and tries to steady her quivering chin. "Would it be okay if we left some of Kim here with Dad?" She shakes her head frantically, trying to quell the surge of her sobs so she doesn't wake the baby. "So when we come see Dad, we can visit them both?" she wails.

My mother's voice is toneless and rigid, yet I can see it's not from indifference, but to hide the wails she herself would like to let out. "Yes, of course, honey. Please leave some of Kim here with Timothy," she whispers.

Bradley kneels down to our father's gravesite. He takes both hands and plunges them into the earth, picking up several fistfuls of dirt and throwing them to the side. He claps his hands together and brown dirt falls from them, but most stays lodged under his fingernails. His shaking hands unthread the cylindrical urn from its cap on the black satin cord necklace and slowly pour some of the ashes into the hole he's made right next to our father's tombstone. I scoot closer to him. Mom hovers over us. He packs a bit of dirt back into the hole, pours more ashes, and packs more earth over his pour. Mom rolls Kimbra's stroller to and fro. Shay takes out her phone, and with a nod to Bradley, asks his permission. Once granted, she takes a photograph.

We sit back and stare at the grave in front of us with the remnants of parents that don't exist. The headstone has my father's name, his birth and death dates, and an inscription that Mom picked out: *Though your song has ended, your music carries on.*

I stare at the words carefully. I've probably seen them dozens of times, but today they really hit different. The thing is, my father's song has not ended. He lives on in his music. And as long as we have his music, we will always have a part of him with us.

Chapter 23
Band Played On

2013

I look out at the beautiful mess of a crowd: an ocean of denim jeans, ripped T-shirts, and excited faces staring back at us—two hundred eleven thousand faces, to be exact. Just offstage stand our families and friends, Bonnie, a few executives from SLZ Media, our old tour manager Logan, the show's promoters, the film crew recording us for the documentary we're making, and a production crew of more than two hundred people. In the parking lot sit thirty-four tractor trailers, a 747 fueling up to fly our equipment to the next venue, and, unlike the old days when we slummed it on a tour bus, a private jet to haul us out of here at the end of the night.

Our stadium tour features complicated set change after complicated set change, each aligning with the era it represents: one set for songs from our old album, one set for the new record, one set for Parker's solo album. There's even a set to replicate Parker's video for "Divide," the song that featured Shay and me making out, the song that started it all, you could say.

Noticeably absent from the side of the stage are our record label's CEO or A&R—and that's because *we* are the CEO and A&R of own record label. With the help of a solid promotional partnership with SLZ Media, we put out an already iconic album, aptly entitled *Magnum Opus*.

The crowd is a force of nature, ready to embrace us, and while my outward facade screams, *Fuck yeah!* my inner monologue keeps repeating, *Damn, this is a lot of people.* The energy is electric. Homemade Pause For Effect banners are everywhere. One by one we take our spots onstage, all of us but Parker, that is. A feedback loop plays out from my amp and Nelson hits the snare once and then again. Shay is in front of her amp, back to the crowd, facing Parker's spot, but Parker is still backstage, looking out at us. I stand stiff, facing the crowd, my guitar hanging low. Parker looks me in the eyes, nods his head. It's time.

Nelson slams his sticks together, a signal to the crowd that we are about to begin. Parker's absence rouses their thunder. I twist the volume knob of my guitar to ten and pluck a few chords with my father's guitar pick. I nod to Shay. She plays the opening line. And with this, the crowd begins chanting loudly, "Pause," "For," "Effect." The drums and bass clang down, Nelson picks up with a rolling snare, the intro swells and we hunker down to the song's opening riff—and just as we do, Parker jumps out as if out of thin air, mic in hand. The crowd is blind with excitement. There are no longer individuals, singing or moving their bodies to the music—they're now a collective being, surging with the melody as one.

Pause For Effect is backed by a stunning display of photographs and a well-choreographed light show. Our set fires up—literally—as flames shoot from the sides of the stage. We hit the chorus, catalyzing another collective flow from the masses.

We're playing "Get Out." It's gritty and fast-paced and wholly inspired by our tug-of-war termination with Four Chords. It took longer than I expected to come to an agreement, for them to let us out of our contract, but in the end, they did. The drama pushed the four of us into the throes of a shared writing affinity. For a while, we only seemed able to put pen to paper to bitch about how much of a swine Bill Sweeney was. We kept his name out of the lyrics, naturally, though anyone with even a modicum of critical thinking skills would be able to piece together what the lyrics "*Stop, stop, stop exploiting us*" are about.

Parker mumbles something borderline unintelligible after our opening song, but not because he's been drinking—for once. He's so lost in the moment that he doesn't care if he makes sense to the crowd. And they love whatever he says. "Everyone here has had their heart broken. Some of you may still be getting your heart broken. You"—he points to an unsuspecting woman in the front row—"may even break a heart tonight." He laughs.

"So, yeah," he concludes. "Pause For Effect is back." Nelson gives Parker an exaggerated drum roll that sets the audience jumping. I look over to Shay, who is tuning her guitar. She smiles and sticks her tongue out at me.

Pause For Effect's distinct brand of indie rock plays out with familiar cadences. Our new tunes are drenched in unrelenting struggles, but we own them, we put them out ourselves. We don't have music industry executives puppeteering us, and this makes all the suffering we've endured worthwhile.

"As much as things change, they really stay the same," Parker jokes in his ever-endearing drawl. He looks behind him to Nelson, and then to Shay, and finally to me. I let a staccato guitar line rip.

The unhinged crowd is fired up for us.

One, two, three, four! The music begins again, fast and pulsating. The final song of our set is the musical equivalent of channeling our inner Jackson Pollack. We thrash and drip sound until a pivotal moment when a feeling comes over us all, commanding us to stop.

As the last chord rings through the speakers, the crowd goes bananas. Our song becomes louder, not because of Parker's singing but because the roar of the crowd crescendos, rendering everything deafening. Shay turns to me with her eyes gleaming and leans in. My guitar and her bass attract each other like magnets. Our onstage kiss makes the whole place explode in screams. We run offstage amid the applause and an enviable amount of stomping and hollering.

• • •

We spend the better part of our days on tour promoting the album. Our final promo stop is at SLZ Media Studio. Sofia Alexi grins from ear to ear to see the entire band back together in front of her. Her audience goes wild as we walk in and take a seat together on her couch.

Sofia directs her first comment right at me. "While the entire album is so personal and vulnerable, I feel like a lot of attention has been given to the best song, 'There's So Much I Need to Say to You.' "

"That's the first song Shay and I wrote together." I blink, in part because the lights in SLZ Media Studio are so bright but also because it's all so surreal that it's almost unbelievable.

"When you write a song," Shay says, "it's like a bit of you exists outside of you."

And that's when it crystalizes for me, the realization that my father's greatest gift to the world is not a hit song— it's me and Gwen, his children.

"Now, music isn't the only legacy you'll leave behind." Sofia looks at Shay and me. This part is well rehearsed, but for the fans' sake we play along as if we're spilling the tea on something exclusive.

"Well." I shift in my seat and face Shay. "Should we tell them?"

The audience hoots and drowns us out with applause.

"Yeah." She nods.

To lessen the gravity of the moment, Shay jokes, "Taryn isn't going to be able to die her hair for a while."

Sofia chuckles a bit.

I sit up a little bit straighter and hold one hand under my abs and another just under my breasts, cupping an invisible full moon on my belly. "We're having a baby," Shay and I say in tandem. Sofia Alexi speaks to the camera that's trained on her. "You heard it here first! Shay and Taryn from Pause For Effect are expecting their first child."

Chapter 24
Adoring You

2014

"There's So Much I Need to Say to You" spent the last thirty-nine weeks on the pop charts, and I've spent as many of those weeks being pregnant. That is, until today.

"There's a time to push, Taryn, and that time is not now." Shay's calmness is both comforting and completely terrifying.

The room hovers, revolves, and rotates with absolutely no regard for my condition. Until now, my only point of reference for what to expect has been my sister's birth, so I already know the nuts and bolts of birth are pretty boring.

Thirteen hours pass and there's finally a shimmer of hope that I might be giving birth soon. The painting of the S-shaped river that adorns the far wall becomes my focal point. Shay talks me through each contraction, reminding me not to fight them but to let myself go. My contractions are coming one on top of another. I find it increasingly difficult to relax. The pressure on my abdomen, as heavy as a brick, violently urges me to push.

For two more hours, I labor. I stand up, I kneel, I make promises to a god I don't believe in, and I simply beg for the strength to continue. Shay maintains her position in my heart as both my rock and my rock star: during each contraction, she rubs my back with tiny massage balls to help ease the pain. She begs me to breathe deeply and assures me that we are almost there. Despite my complaints and choice words, she stays firm, ever my star.

I release guttural moans like a wounded animal to get through the pain. While knowing what is going on physiologically makes me less scared, nothing—absolutely nothing—makes this less painful. Focusing on my breath isn't doing shit. I am on the verge of admitting that I was wrong for not taking the drugs.

"The harder this is, the closer you are," Shay repeats.

I throw a cup of ice across the room. "Make it fucking end," I howl.

"Take it one contraction at a time, and we will get through it," she says calmly, and I spray expletives like Don Corleone sprayed bullets in *The Godfather*, all over the room, at any person willing to make eye contact with me.

A doctor finally enters the room. She's about five feet tall and introduces herself. "Hi, I'm Juliet."

Juliet starts making small talk. "I know your band." She starts humming out the chorus of our latest single.

"I'll write a song about you if you get this goddamn kid out of me," I growl.

She finally tells me I am allowed to push.

I sit up in bed and endeavor to crush my organs in ways that will allow an actual human to emerge from me. I push as long and as hard as I can. As the baby's head crowns, Shay coaches me like I'm Hope Solo at the World Cup. At 9:18 p.m., our darling son is placed on my belly. With tears in her eyes, Shay announces that we have a baby boy, Timothy Taylor Hughes. He is beautiful: his body pink, his eyes closed, and his mouth screaming, just like my father's guitar did in so many of his hit songs.

• • •

About an hour later, our guests begin pouring in. Mom leans in and kisses me on the forehead.

"Isn't he beautiful?" Gwen coos, elbowing Bradley as they look down and admire him.

"He's beautiful," Bradley replies.

Shay makes her way around the room, kissing everyone hello.

"Where's Kimbra?" Mom asks Gwen.

"Oh, she's with PJ."

"Oh, that's nice," Mom says to Bradley. PJ is his cousin. Bradley's made a concerted effort to dig deeper into the remaining relationships he has with his family since Kimbra was born.

"Kimbra goes wild for PJ," Gwen adds.

"She wants no part of us when PJ's around." Bradley laughs.

"She's not going to come today?" I murmur to no one in particular.

Shay brushes my hair to the side. "Yes, Gwen texted us last night, honey. You were a bit preoccupied, though."

Shay announces to everyone, "The birth was amazing."

"The birth was painful," I temper.

"Soddy hell, look at him, he's beautiful," Nelson says as he attempts to quietly close the door of my room, but Parker's right behind him.

"Now admit it, all the pain was worth it, right?" Mom asks.

"It's like comparing a Slash guitar solo to the entire Vitamin String Quartet."

"I don't understand you, honey. Are those rappers you're referring to?"

Shay laughs and walks over to greet Nelson and Parker. "She's saying that there's no comparison," she tells Mom. "He was worth the pain."

"Did you see the baby?" I ask everyone.

"I've already taken a selfie holding him and posted it to Facebook," Mom says.

"Mom!" I protest. "I don't want him on the internet."

"Well," she shrugs, "too late."

I let it go, too tired to argue with her on the dangers of chronicling every moment of a kid's life on the internet. It seems too ironic, even if I do mean it, being that we're famous and that the minutiae of our lives are already broadcast on the daily.

Through half-shut eyelids, I observe Shay and Mom ogling Timothy. Mom is asking Shay for the exact time of his birth so she can "read his birth chart." Shay and Nelson video chat with their father and Bethany to show them the baby but don't stay on too long. It's nearly 4 a.m. in London.

I raise my arms and Shay puts Timothy on my chest so that he can latch onto me for a feeding. My adrenaline's whizzing but I secretly fantasize about sleeping. My mind illuminates with the memory of Timothy's first wail. My heart swells as I recall Shay's face as she first laid eyes on our boy. The pillow rustles a bit as I slowly lift my head off it. The sound of Timothy's breathing is the background to my moments, a soundtrack to which only Shay and I are attuned. Life is complicated. It's not black and white. It's not linear. And it's often unfair. But this moment, holding my brand-new baby in my arms, is uncomplicated. It's fair. It's the only moment that matters. The beginning of the rest of my life starts right here.

"You going to snip his penis?" Parker asks.

"Please don't talk about his penis," Shay warns. She and I turn to each other, acknowledging the irony in defending a penis.

I try to keep up with their conversations, but I can't pull my eyes off Timothy. He looks up at me, and I look down at him, and everything else falls out of focus.

"Is Mommy allergic to flowers?" a nurse asks as she walks into the room.

I motion my head toward Shay.

"No, she's not allergic," Shay says as she takes the flowers from the nurse.

"No card." The nurse adds.

"They're Passion Flowers." Gwen catches the nurse just after she's left the room and pulls her back in.

"Actually, turns out, Mommy is allergic to *these* flowers." Gwen puts the vase into the nurse's hand. "You can have them."

"Oh, they're beautiful. I'll leave them on the nurse's station. Will they bother Mommy out here at the nurse's station?"

There's just something wrong about speaking about yourself in the third person, but I stop the nurse in her tracks, "No, they won't bother Mommy in here, they can stay."

Gwen shrugs.

Mom pushes the pillow behind me under my back so I can sit up. She straightens the pillow again, and I shift a little more to face Shay.

"Will the flowers bother you?"

"Why would they bother me?" Shay asks.

"Passion Flowers are Violette's signature flower." Gwen responds before I can.

Shay glances down at Timothy and back up at me. She holds my gaze for a beat, "The flowers can stay."

Across the street, two landscapers with noisy leaf blowers send a swirl of green and amber leaves off in a procession to the curb. A man jogs past, his sneakers pressing against the same leaves, and a taxi slows to a halt to let the jogger cross the street. It's amazing how once a baby enters the world, the most innocuous actions crystallize just how vulnerable even the simplest of moments can be.

I rub my hand against Timothy's tiny fingers and tell him, "I am going to teach you about the music business, and your other mommy is going to teach you about the right light to take an impeccable photograph." A tender smile crosses Shay's face. "And Parker's going to teach you how to sing from your head *and* your chest, and your Aunty Gwen"—I look around the room—"is going to teach you how to wear eyeliner?" I say as if it's a question.

Mom, ever the psychologist, says, "It's totally fine. We don't care if he wears makeup."

I continue, "And Bradley will teach you how to ride a motorcycle."

Shay overrides this idea. "Maybe just a bicycle."

"And Nelson is going to teach you everything you need to know about banging on a drum."

We have all, each of us, loved and lost: a mother, a father, a husband. I remind myself not to just focus on what they left us, but who their absence inspired us to become. These losses spur us to live up to our greatest potential, to realize our ambitions, to live despite our fears. Mom has always bragged that the greatest accomplishment of her life is her children—but I can't help but wonder if her most meaningful feat is how deeply she loved my father.

Timothy removes himself from my breast and spits up a little. I wipe it up with my pajama shirt, and then he latches back on. I look around the room at my people: my family, my chosen family, the ones I love most.

"I cannot wait for you to be old enough to understand me, Timothy. There's so much I need to say to you."

Nelson sings: "*You got what you wanted from me.*"

Shay joins in: "*And I got what I needed.*"

Parker pipes up: "*You never let me speak my truth.*"

And I whisper: "*And now we're both in pieces.*"

There are smiles all around.

You cannot go to the grocery store, get in a cab, or scroll through a music streaming playlist without hearing Pause For Effect's hit anthem. All of us, even Mom, belt out the chorus and sing, in perfect harmony: "*There's so much I need to say to you.*"

The critics aren't the only ones saying it's our best song—we believe it too.

Thanks, Dad.

Acknowledgments

Thank you:

Sonia, for your endless love and support and for making me laugh every damn day. Bash, for inspiring me to be the best version of myself. Mom, for making the mundane absolutely riotous, and Lila, for indulging her Peggy-isms. Wendy and Catherine, I still can't believe I've tricked you two into this many years of friendship. Diana, for editing numerous drafts of this book—I am forever grateful to you. Naz, for being as close to a sister-in-law that I am going to get. Dee, for so many solid years of friendship, but especially for always being down to play Clue. Jenna and Patty for being the "pick up where we left off" friends. Marita, for being one of the warmest humans to ever grace my presence. Mia, for always having my back. Abel, for that funny line about the Germans that I unabashedly stole. Debbie, for always making sure I am represented on the Christmas tree. Alberto, for being you. The Murderinos, especially Karen and Georgia, and my very own IRL murderino friend, Kate. Dr. Tony Ortega, Renee, Liz, Maryellen, Steph, Matthew, Lauren, Gabbie, Jennie "Kathleen Mary" Vega, Chris Wlach, Tony, Bertini, Max Wyeth, Shannon, Melissa, Kyra, Madalena, Ken, Nico, and Marley. Predrag Marković for the brilliant cover art. The team at FriesenPress for providing solid support every step of the way. Go-Kart Records and the Lunachicks for igniting this fire inside me, all those years ago.

CPSIA information can be obtained
at www.ICGtesting.com
Printed in the USA
BVHW070929290921
617681BV00005B/541